Yaqui Delgado Wants to Kick Your Ass

Yaqui Delgado Wants to Kick Your Ass

MEG MEDINA

CANDLEWICK PRESS

Copyright © 2013 by Margaret Medina

First edition 2013

Library of Congress Catalog Card Number 2012943645
ISBN 978-0-7636-5859-5

13 14 15 16 17 BVG 10 9 8 7 6 5 4 3 2

Printed in Berryville, VA, U.S.A.

This book was typeset in ITC Giovanni.

Candlewick Press
99 Dover Street
Somerville, Massachusetts 02144

visit us at www.candlewick.com

CHAPTER 1

"Yaqui Delgado wants to kick your ass."

A kid named Vanesa tells me this in the morning before school. She springs out with no warning and blocks my way, her textbook held at her chest like a shield. She's tall like me and caramel. I've seen her in the lunchroom, I think. Or maybe just in the halls. It's hard to remember.

Then, just like that, Vanesa disappears into the swell of bodies all around.

Wait, I want to tell her as she's swallowed up. *Who is Yaqui Delgado?* But instead, I stand there blinking as kids jostle for the doors. The bell has rung, and I'm not sure if it's only the warning or if I'm late for first period. Not that it matters. I've been at this school for five weeks, and Mr. Fink hasn't remembered to take attendance once. A girl near his desk just sort of scans the room and marks who's out.

"Move, idiot!" somebody grunts, and I follow the crowd inside.

It's Darlene Jackson who explains the trouble I'm really in. She's a student aide in the guidance office, and she knows all about Yaqui Delgado. "She was suspended last year for fighting." We're in the lunchroom, so Darlene has to shout for me to hear. *"Twice."*

I've only known Darlene a few weeks, but already I can tell she loves drama, especially if she has a front-row seat and it's someone else's catastrophe. Her mother is one of those nosy PTA types, too, so Darlene always seems to know whose parents are getting divorced, who failed last semester, or what teacher will be fired at the end of the year. Don't ask me how, but that little spy even knew that our science teacher's husband had dumped her. Before Ms. O'Donnell got past her swollen eyes to teach us about Newton's laws last week, the whole class knew her love life was in shambles.

Darlene pushes up her glasses and tells me the whole rumor: "Yaqui Delgado hates you. She says you're stuck-up for somebody who just showed up out of nowhere. And she wants to know who the hell you think you are, shaking your ass the way you do." Darlene lowers her voice. "She even called you a *skank*. Sorry."

I'm stunned.

"I shake my ass?"

2

Darlene studies her egg-salad sandwich for a second. "Definitely, yes."

Interesting. I've only had an ass for about six months, and now it seems it has a mind of its own. If only my friend Mitzi were here to see this! Last year in ninth grade at my old school, I was a late bloomer. *Planchadita* — ironed out and hipless — nothing at all like Mitzi, who got her curves in fifth grade.

It was Ma who first noticed my body changing, but she wasn't exactly tactful about my getting *cuerpo.* "Put on a bra already, Piddy," she said after she noticed a man on the bus gawking at my chest one day. "You can't go around with two loose onions in your shirt for all the boys to stare at," she snapped, like it was my fault that man had helped himself to the show.

Lila — that's Ma's best friend in the whole world — is the one who took me shopping for lacy bras the next day.

"Be proud, *mi vida,*" Lila whispered to me in the bra section of the store as I stared, shocked, at all the lace and bows. "And keep your shoulders back."

This ass shaking is probably Lila's fault, now that I think about it. It's all the dancing we do. She's been teaching me to merengue the way they do in her favorite clubs. Right before school started, she introduced me to her collection of old Héctor Lavoe records. We've listened to them so much that I've got the tunes stuck in my head.

"Move your feet small, like you're on a brick," she said when we danced across her apartment. "But the hips? Shake them big, *mami*." She gave her bottom a good one-two to show me. *"Así."*

Maybe now I'm stuck on swivel. Who knows? When Lila walks down the street, men's eyes get glued to her junk. Even bus drivers slow down to see. Ma says she's a human traffic hazard.

Darlene finishes nibbling down to her crusts and tosses them inside her paper lunch bag.

"Maybe you could practice walking normal," she suggests with a shrug. "You know, a little less wiggly. Like me."

I try not to choke. Darlene does not *walk normal*. She leans forward as if she's being led by her nose with an invisible rope. I'd say she scurries.

"I think I walk just fine," I tell her.

"Suit yourself, then," she says. "All I know is that Yaqui Delgado is gonna crush you." She demonstrates by balling up her lunch bag and casting a knowing glance at the table across the lunchroom. That's where the Latin kids sit.

The first day I got here, I stood with my tray, just sizing up the neighborhood. The Asian kids were clustered near the middle. The black kids had a bunch of tables to themselves. I spotted the Latin zone right away, but I didn't know a single one of them from any of my classes. As I got closer, a few of the guys grinned and elbowed each other, but none of the girls looked like they were going to make

4

room. In fact, it was downright chilly how they stared at me. Luckily, Darlene waved me over.

So here I am at the corner table near the trash cans — the worst real estate in the cafeteria. Since we moved, I've had to start over. Our table is all the kids from our fourth-period science class, like Sally Ngyuen and Rob Allen. They're both in the tenth-grade physics class with Darlene and me, which I'm finding out is a breeding ground for outcasts here at Daniel Jones High School.

Right now Rob is looking scared — even for him. He's not an ugly guy, but he's skinny and pale. The knot in his neck is bobbing, and the rims of his eyes look as pink as a hamster's. He's crazy smart, which I like, though he might be more popular if his brain came in a more attractive package. He can solve a physics problem even faster than I can, but what does that get him around here? Not a single friend that I can see — and I would know. His locker is next to mine.

"Who's going to crush you?" His voice cracks a little as he stares at the balled-up paper bag.

"No one," I say.

"Mind your own business, Rob," Darlene snaps. She turns back to me and rolls her eyes. Even in a group of geeks, there's a pecking order, and Darlene's on top. Rob glares at her, but he shuts up.

"I don't even know Yaqui Delgado, Darlene," I tell her with a shrug. "I'm not worried."

5

"Well, she knows *you*. And she hates your guts. You're new here, Piddy, so take my word for it. You're as good as dead. These Latin girls mean business. If I were you, I'd stay home tomorrow."

I stop chewing and give her a look.

"In case you haven't noticed, I'm a Latin girl, too, Darlene."

Darlene rolls her eyes — *again* — like I'm the stupid one. White-skinned. No accent. Good in school. I'm not her idea of a Latina at all. I could point out that Cameron Diaz is Latina, too, but why bother? It won't change Darlene's mind.

"Yeah? Then why aren't you sitting with them?" she asks.

The color rises in my cheeks as my eyes flit across the room. It's because those girls are a rougher bunch — nothing at all like Mitzi and me. Still, I won't give Darlene the satisfaction of knowing that. It's bad enough that when Coach Malone read out my last name in PE and the Guatemalan girls in back gave me weird looks, even though they should know better. "You Spanish?" they asked. I ignored them.

"My last name is *Sanchez*, remember?" I finally say to Darlene. "My mother is from Cuba, and my dad is from the Dominican Republic. I'm just as Latin as they are."

I finish off my peanut-butter sandwich and force myself to make small talk with Rob for the rest of lunch period, just to annoy her. This is harder than it might seem. He's not much of what you'd call a conversationalist; I think he's out of practice. His thoughts more or less explode from his mouth without warning.

"I'm going to make a dagger," he blurts out.

It takes me a second to realize he's talking about our English project. We're starting to work on our *Julius Caesar* presentations.

"Watch out for 'zero tolerance,' " I tell him. "I know a kid who got suspended for a water pistol in sixth grade." It was my neighbor Joey Halper, early in his career as a goon.

Rob shrugs.

"I'll say it's Reynolds Wrap before I whip it out."

"Creeper. What are you whipping out?" Darlene sneers.

Rob turns red, and that pretty much ends our chat. Thankfully, the bell rings just then, and we join the stampede for the door. I can't help but look over my shoulder at those girls. I don't see Vanesa, but maybe one of them is Yaqui. Maybe she's watching me right now, staring at my swishy ass, hating me. I hold my books tight and press forward in the crowd, keeping my hips as still as I can.

CHAPTER 2

How I got into this *lío* at Daniel Jones High is because the lobby staircase in our old apartment building finally gave way, and Ma said, *"¡Hasta aquí!"* Otherwise, I'd be at Charles P. Jeantet on the better side of Northern Boulevard, and nobody would be after me at all.

But every week, something would happen in the building to rattle Ma. No hot water from the boiler on Mondays. Mr. and Mrs. Halper fighting so bad, Lila sometimes called the cops. Dog turd from the old boxer in 1D that's ninety-one in people years and can't make it outside in time anymore. It was all getting on Ma's nerves — not exactly her strong point — and that day when the stairs went *pfft,* she'd worked overtime, too.

I was in Lila's living room, watching our soap opera, when we heard the crash. It sounded like a *whoosh* followed by a truckload of china breaking. The front door even shook a little. Then came Ma's screams.

"*¡Dios mío! ¿Qué es esto?* Help!"

Lila grabbed the old plunger handle she keeps in case of burglars, and we headed out the door. Sure enough, there was Ma, standing in a cloud of genie smoke, knee-deep in rubble where the five lobby steps had crumbled right under her feet. Covered in all that marble dust, she looked like a Greek statue of herself, only furious, the way you'd picture Medusa. Her hands were shaking; the veins in her neck were ropes. Even after we dug her out and got her upstairs, I could tell she wanted blood.

"*¡Sin vergüenza!* We can't live like animals! We're decent," she shouted into the heating pipe. It ran down the stack of apartments, all the way to the super's place near the laundry room. She smacked a frying pan again and again against the metal to make sure he heard her over the hum of the dryers. Hearing Ma wasn't going to be a problem, of course. The whole building was probably listening in on her *escándalo* through the pipes; maybe even the whole block could hear. That tells you how mad she was, because if there's one thing Ma hates, it's looking low. The worst thing you can be is a *chusma*. She thinks we get a bad rap as Latinos, which she's always trying to undo by being extra quiet and polite all the time.

"Calm yourself, Clara." Lila adjusted the flame under the teakettle and opened up the cupboard to look for honey. "You want a heart attack?"

9

"I don't want to calm down!" Ma's face was nearly purple.

"What if someone calls the cops on us?" I asked, trying to help. What's more *chusma* than *that*, right? It got Ma's attention.

She gave the pipes one more smack before tossing the frying pan aside. Then she flopped into a kitchen chair, exhausted. She tilted her head back and closed her eyes to send a prayer to *el Señor*, though who knows if he still listens to her. It's been fifteen years since she's gone to church. When she opened her eyes again, it was like the irises had been drained of their color and all that was left was steely silver. Her voice was low.

"No, I don't want a heart attack, Lila. And, no, I don't want cops. What I *want* is to move. The Ortegas are lucky they got out when they did." The Ortegas are Mitzi's parents. They moved to Long Island in May to get away from the "bad element" in our neighborhood.

Oh, no, I thought. Not this again. Ma is always threatening to move when she's upset about something—but it's never anywhere reasonable, like Maspeth or Ridgewood. It's always Hialeah or Miami, or should I say, *Me-ah-me,* aka Cuba with food. Sometimes she goes so far as to make us start packing. Once she got so annoyed about the icy walkway out front that she brought home boxes from work and announced that we were leaving for Florida. Luckily, we're the only Cubans in the United States who don't have relatives there, so we wouldn't have had anywhere to stay. Lila found her a good pair of rubber-soled boots on sale instead, and we stayed put.

I had to think fast.

"Mitzi says Long Island isn't so great. The people are snobs." It's a lie. I talked to her last week. She likes it fine, even with the all-girl Catholic high school that came with the deal. "Why don't we just sue the super?" Even this seemed easier than packing up the apartment in boxes — and Ma likes court shows. "Who knows? We could get rich if you're hurt. Do you have a limp? Are you traumatized?"

Ma gave me an exasperated look and turned back to Lila.

"I'm serious. It's not just talk like the other times. And if you don't believe me, look."

She got up, opened the cupboard, and reached for an old El Pico coffee can from the top shelf. When she opened it, I gasped. Inside was a drug-dealer-size wad of bills.

"Ma!" I said. "Did you rob a bank?"

"Don't be fresh. I've been saving," she continued. "And now it's finally time. Lila, get me the phone number for Mr. Wu."

Lila stared at the money and didn't say a word. Mr. Wu is her old boyfriend — a Chinese guy who grew up in

Uruguay—but he's also the owner of Happiness Home Realty, the biggest real-estate agency in this part of Queens.

Ma meant business.

So, Lila set the whole thing up, just like Ma wanted. All she had to promise was a dinner with Mr. Wu, and he said, "*¿Cómo no, linda?* I'll be happy to show your friend what I got." Like I said, no man can resist Lila.

The next day, the three of us were standing with Mr. Wu in front of a two-family house at the corner of Forty-fifth and Parsons Boulevard, not too far from our old place. A FOR RENT sign was taped inside the empty window on the second floor, Mr. Wu's smiling picture overlooking the bus stop.

Mr. Wu was grinning at Lila stupidly as he fumbled for the keys to the apartment. It had been at least six months since Lila had called it quits with him, but I could tell he was hopeful, like all her old boyfriends are for a while afterward. I tried not to notice him practically drooling. Men just get weird around her, like the air gets electric and they go blind to everything except for her. Lila wears heels and sells Avon part-time, when she's not doing *champú* at Salón Corazón. She's nothing like Ma, who is Hanes brief three-packs and a worried face. Lila's hair never shows roots, and when she walks by, it's all Jean Naté and talcum that makes men want to cling to her tighter than her sweaters.

"Too bad she's loose," Ma says when she hears Lila's pumps clicking down the stairs for a date in the city. I don't think she means it — or if she does, it doesn't stop her from loving Lila. I know because I can see the worry lines cutting deep between her eyebrows as we watch Lila through the blinds. Some nights I turn over and find the other side of the sofa bed empty and Ma still waiting at the window for Lila to come home.

Lila isn't bad, though. She's just alive in a way that Ma is too tired to remember. It's like Lila can still hear the rhythm in a salsa on the radio and not just complain about the noise.

"Bonito, right?" Mr. Wu tried yet another key and jutted his chin at the rosebushes hanging over the chain-link fence. It had been a warm September, so they were still pushing up blooms. I nodded to be polite, but it didn't make the place look any better to me. The house looked too quiet. It had no stoop for people to gather on. Nobody was playing out front. And it had those white scrolled bars on the window that scream, *Break-ins happen here!*

Lila circled my waist.

"Only a block away from the school," she whispered in my ear.

"That's a selling point?" I asked.

"Okay, maybe not, but at least it's a short walk."

I could see Daniel Jones High clearly from the front

door. The school takes up half a block and is painted the pale green of disinfectant. There are grates on the windows and blacktop with a long cement wall covered in drawings and neon tags: *Julius 174. 10-ass-itty. Slinky.* Art and barrio all mixed in.

"Here we are!" With a click and a bow, Mr. Wu finally threw open the door. "Utilities included, too, *señoras.*"

He stared at Lila's butt the whole way up to the second floor.

Nothing deterred Ma. Not the ugly blue rug with the mysterious dark stain that I pointed out. Not the dead roaches turning to dust inside the cabinets. Not Mrs. Boika, a nasty Romanian lady downstairs who stared at us without even saying, *¿Hola, qué tal?* or anything. Not even when I asked her how we would move her scratched-up piano from our place to this. It's an upright Steinway that hasn't been tuned in all the years we've had it, but suddenly I was protective.

"It's not like in the cartoons, you know, where movers lower it out a window," I said. Ma ignored me — was she planning to leave it behind after all these years? I wondered — and said the new apartment was perfect. There was a bus stop right outside the door — and no loud neighbors or slobbering dogs to make a mess of things.

"Those were her exact words," I told Mitzi on the phone. "'It's perfect.'" I was sitting on our fire escape later

14

that day, miserable. In the summer, Mitzi and I used to paint our nails out here. Now I picked paint chips off the metal and dropped them over the edge.

"Maybe you'll like it better," she said. "You never know."

"Be serious. I'm switching schools in September of sophomore year. The new place has barred windows. I won't know anybody. How is that 'perfect'?"

Silence.

"Are you still there?" I asked.

"Yeah, sorry. At least school just started, right? Anyway, I need to work on this stupid lab report for physics."

I sighed. A five-alarm fire wouldn't get between Mitzi and her homework. Her dad was a doctor in Honduras, even though here he only works in the lab at a clinic. He has plans for Mitzi to be a surgeon. She'll probably like it, though. She's the only kid I know who didn't make naked Ken and Barbie kiss. Instead, she would amputate their limbs with blunt-edge scissors, their putty-colored little feet lined up on the front stoop.

"What time is it?" she said. Papers shuffled in the background. "*¡Ay!* I gotta go to practice."

"Practice for what?" I asked.

"I'm playing badminton for school."

"The game with the little net thing? That's a *sport*?"

"Yeah, can you believe it? And I suck."

"So why are you doing it?"

"Why else? Mami wants me to make friends."

This made us both laugh. Mitzi has always been kind of shy, her mother's exact opposite. It got really bad when the boys in our class went insta-stupid over Mitzi's boobs in elementary school. After that, it was me who had to tell the boys to shut their filthy mouths — and ask for the movie tickets and the explanation for the homework, too.

"You coming to Queens soon?" I didn't want to say *I miss you* because she already knew that.

"The first weekend that I don't have a game. Maybe we can go shopping for your birthday present."

I couldn't answer through the tight feeling in my throat.

"Look, Piddy, don't worry. It's going to be okay," Mitzi said before we hung up. "Take it from me. You can't do anything about moving, anyway, so try to make the best of it. Besides, people always like you. You're going to kick butt."

I was already missing Lila as the three of us packed up our old kitchen a week later. I was sitting at the piano bench, plucking at the stuck keys.

"*Ay,* Clara, tell this kid to stop with the sad face; she's breaking my heart." Lila taped newspaper around two plates and kissed my forehead. "Your *mami's* right. You can't stay here." She wiped the lipstick off my skin with her handkerchief and tucked it back inside her bra. "The whole place is turning to dust."

Ma looked up and frowned at me.

"Piddy, stop that racket and help us. And quit moping. You should be thankful." She yanked tape over a box of pots. "The new apartment's not far, and — did you see? — it even has a yard."

I gave her a stony stare.

"That patch of dirt?"

"It has *roses*," she said. "You can sit outside with a new friend from school and smell their perfume," she continued. "That's good for a young girl."

"*Ay*, Ma . . ." I muttered.

"'*Ay*, Ma,' what?" she mimicked.

I sighed.

Ma is always inventing endless things that are "good for a young girl" — which means, specifically, me. Hemming pants. Washing out underwear by hand because "What decent woman puts her private things in a public washer?" Learning to fry chicken so it isn't bloody near the bone. Speaking rudimentary French. Cross-stitching pillows — I kid you not — so I'll know how to stitch my baby's initials into its bibs someday. All sorts of pointless things that are supposed to improve me "for the future."

Too bad I have other plans in mind.

Ma doesn't know it, but I'm going to be a scientist. I

want to work with animals, big ones like elephants, maybe even live halfway across the world. It's weird, I know. The only elephants I've ever seen were in the zoo. But we have the National Geographic channel, so I know they're smart and they can feel and hear things people can't. They can keep a herd's whole history — all the good and the bad they've ever seen — in their memory. If I told this to Ma, her screams would touch the sky. *"¿Elefantes?"* She'd nag about malaria and the smell of dung I'd never get out from under my nails. She'd ask me what kind of decent girl is interested in elephants. And so on.

It's times like these I wish I were Lila's daughter instead. Not that Ma doesn't love me — or that Lila likes elephants. It's just that Lila doesn't *bother* me. She's never had kids of her own, thank God, so she doesn't have the slightest idea of what's good for me. She doesn't ask me if I've done my homework or where I've been. When Ma works late, we fill up on butter cookies for dinner and watch the good shows that Ma calls trash. If I were Lila's kid, life might actually be fun.

"Forget smelling flowers," Lila said. "A pretty girl like you? Boys will be sending you roses of your own!" Then she wiggled her eyebrows. "The good news is you'll have your own room. Just think, now you'll have *privacy.* Every sixteen-year-old girl needs that."

"She's not sixteen yet," Ma muttered.

"A few weeks . . ." Lila said, winking.

I looked around at the packed boxes and felt my throat go dry. I already hated the new apartment and Daniel Jones High School. I hadn't felt this bad since Mitzi's moving van pulled away from our street.

But I held my tongue. Getting my own room *was* the only shining piece of good news in this whole thing. It meant I wouldn't have to share a sofa bed with Ma, who snores and takes my covers. Still, the "pretty" part was ridiculous. I've never been one of the pretty girls. Mitzi's the good-looking one, all curvy like a guitar. I'm tall and skinny. My eyes are wide set and the color of mud. Joey Halper says I look like a toad, presumably now one with a booty. Sometimes he croaks *ribbit* from his window when he sees me outside and wants to say hello.

"That's right," Ma said. "Your own room. No more lumpy sofa bed." She paused over a bowl with a melted rim. "Maybe now you won't slouch."

Through the window, I could see the empty lot next door and the bowl of milk I had left there that morning. I moved the jade elephant on my chain back and forth nervously. Sometimes the sound of my necklace makes me feel calm.

"What's going to happen to the kittens?" I asked. The mother tabby I'd been feeding near the cellar had been roaming with a low belly for days. She'd grown to the size of a raccoon. The litter would come any day. I thought of what could happen without me: dogs, the cold, rotten kids, even the super with a shovel. He's an idiot that way.

"Cats are wild at heart, *mi amor*. They figure out how to survive." Lila came to the window and closed her hand around my cold fingers. "Now, give me a hug. Good things are waiting for you, Piddy. I promise."

CHAPTER 3

My key is stuck in the lock. Again. At the old place, Lila had a spare key whenever I needed it. Here I'm on my own. The weather turned cold today, chilly enough outside to make my nose run and my fingers feel stiff. It takes me five minutes of jiggling and pushing to get the lock to release.

Mrs. Boika watches me from her perch behind her kitchen window as if I'm a burglar. If she didn't blink every so often, I'd swear she was already dead and stuffed, like one of Lila's customers did to her pet Chihuahua, complete with glass eyeballs and everything.

The steps to our apartment are right beside the old bat's back door in the hall. It takes all I've got not to give her door a good kick.

"Hello, Mrs. Boika," I call, just to point out her rudeness. She doesn't respond.

I climb the steps and unlock our door. Nobody is home, of course. It's Friday, and Ma will be at Attronica until nine tonight. She works in the shipping department, where lifting flat-screen TVs is killing her. A person's back can only take so much, she says. Tonight I'll have to rub her shoulders with Iodex until the whole apartment smells of wintergreen and my hands are shiny with oil. If this isn't a pathetic life, I don't know what is. I can't even talk to Mitzi to tell her what happened and see what she thinks. She's trapped at her cousin's house in New Jersey until Saturday, so I text her instead.

Having an ass problem, I type.

?? You have an ass? Call me Sat pm! Gotta go.

The apartment is still cluttered with half-emptied moving boxes that I kick out of my way to get to the kitchen. Ma and I work at unpacking every day, but somehow it's like new boxes spring up overnight, and we never seem to finish. Who knew we owned so much junk? Worse, nothing is labeled. That was Lila's job; we should have known better. She got distracted and forgot. "I can't think when I'm emotional," she explained. So now everything we unpack is a surprise. When we need something, we arm ourselves with a box cutter and go hunting as though we're at the flea market on a Saturday morning. Two nights ago, I found my old CDs mixed with my winter coats in the bathroom. Ma unearthed the teakettle in her bedroom.

I grab a cereal bar from the kitchen and head back to my room, music piping through my headphones. It still smells of roach spray and fresh paint in here, compliments

22

of the landlord. I prop open the window with my wooden ruler and throw myself on the bed. It's all I've got in here besides the ugly dresser that Ma and Lila dragged home on Large Trash Day.

I can't get Yaqui Delgado out of my mind. Plenty of girls shake their junk. How is that enough to make somebody hate you? It's crazy.

I turn up the music to chase Yaqui out of my head, and dig out my English notebook. Naturally, I can't find a pen to use for my homework. I'm sure there are some in a box somewhere. Time to go hunting.

Boxes are stacked everywhere on the upright piano and its bench to form a kind of mountain. Not that it matters. Ma is the only one who can play, and she says she never has time. Still, she gave the moving guys fifty bucks extra to drag it up these stairs.

"If you don't play it, why should we bring it?" I asked.

"A piano makes a house looks classy," she snapped.

I grab a box from near the foot pedals and find Ma's old handbags and shoes, even a little beaded evening bag I've never seen before. The next box has old phone and rent bills folded neatly inside plastic bags. It's Ma's extensive bookkeeping, down to the last penny. Then I find loose photographs. For a minute, I don't reach for them. Looking at old pictures sucks me in — and not in a good, nostalgic way. Most people feel happy looking at old photos. Me? I just feel lost and jumbled. For all of Ma's organization and bookkeeping, she's never figured out a way to keep pictures straight. Pictures are supposed to tell your story, but our story looks like it doesn't make sense. I dig my arms in almost up to my elbows and pull one free. Ma and Lila toasting Cokes to the camera. They're young and laughing. You can see they're good friends. I dig in again and pull free a class picture: Mitzi and me in Mrs. Resnick's class, me with oversized front teeth, standing by our diorama, the best one in the class. Another dig and I pull free a fuzzy shot of us at Rockaway Beach under a striped umbrella with Mr. and Mrs. Ortega. Again, and I find an old one of me in a high chair with smashed-up tamales on my cheeks.

I play this game for way too long; it's almost dark by the time I stretch my legs and stand up. If Ma knew what I was doing, she'd be mad. "What are you looking for?" she'd snap, even though she knows the answer: a picture of my father. Ma and Lila made sure there was no evidence left with the help of a Bic lighter. I could dig to China, and I won't find any photos of him. It's like he never existed at all.

I close the box and give it a little shove into the corner. Then I smash my fingers along the piano keys as loudly as I can. *Hello, Mrs. Boika! Like the tune?*

The pens, I suddenly remember, are in the box with the Ajax beside the bathroom.

"The trouble probably isn't your ass. I'll bet it's a guy."
Mitzi holds up a shirt. We're shopping on Sunday. She's got
thirty dollars, she says, enough for my birthday present —
elephant earrings! — *and* a new shirt if she's careful. "My
God, I'm so sick of my uniform, and it's only October," she
mutters, putting the shirt back.

Almost as soon as she got off the N-16 bus this morning, I told Mitzi what Vanesa said and about the lunchroom tables. I even walked ahead of her down the street
so she could tell me the truth about my walk. On a scale
of one to ten, she gave me a seven in shake. I stare over the
rack and wrinkle my nose.

"What's that supposed to mean?"

"You ever wear knee-length polyester all day?"

"Not that. What do you mean 'a guy'? There are no
guys in this picture."

"Yeah, sure. That's what *you* think." She sounds a little
sad when she says it. A boy hasn't looked Mitzi in the eyes
for years. Their eyes stay glued to her chest. "I'll bet her
boyfriend noticed you or something stupid like that. But if
that's what happened, you're done."

"That's not my fault. Jesus, I don't even know what *she*
looks like."

"So find out."

"Creep on her?"

"Exactly."

"How am I going to do that?"

Mitzi cocks her head and gives me a look.

"*¡Por favor!* Use your brain. Nobody's a match for that." She pulls out another shirt. This one is loose and roomy the way she likes. "Ooh. *Now* we're in business."

We share a dressing room. I try on a clingy blue dress in an African pattern while she tries on the shirt. The whole time I'm thinking about the boys at the lunch table. Maybe Mitzi is right. Maybe one of them actually noticed me. Stranger things have happened.

"What do you think?" I say, stepping out and circling in front of the mirror. It's not a little-kid dress, that's for sure. Ma would take one look and say something about short skirts and immorality.

"Perfect," she says.

"You ladies finding everything all right?" the store manager asks, smiling. He's pretty old — like thirty or something — but he's cute. Mitzi flushes and stares at her shoes.

"We're fine, thanks," I tell him.

Mitzi grabs my arm as we head out a few minutes later with our bags. The manager waves through the window.

"Behold the devastating power of your new booty," she tells me, sighing.

I give her a shove. Laughing, we run all the way down the street.

CHAPTER 4

I read somewhere about a mathematician who said he could solve difficult equations in his sleep. He claimed that his subconscious could figure out problems he couldn't solve when he was awake.

I'm not a genius, but it must work like that for me, too.

When I wake up on Monday, I have a perfect plan for stalking Yaqui.

"Where are you going so early?" Ma asks as I zip up my sweatshirt at the door. "I made you eggs."

"School," I say, holding up the cereal bar I snatched for my pocket. "There's a club meeting."

Ma looks so happy, I almost feel bad about lying. The truth is that the only people who get to DJ early are the ones eating the free breakfast. Me? I won't spend a minute more at school than I have to. In this case, though, it's better that she thinks I go to a school like Mitzi's, where people practically live full-time.

"What club?" Ma asks.

"Library." I hustle out the door before there are any more questions.

Nobody much is in the school yard when I get there, except for a few guys hanging near the fence. I recognize a couple of them from the forbidden Latin lunch table. I walk fast, trying not to be noticed, but, of course, they have to go out of their way to call me out.

"Move that junk, *mami!*" one of them calls, making squeezing motions with his hands. I don't turn around to give him the finger, though I probably should. Instead, I hurry up the steps two at a time.

The library looks deserted as usual. The only time I've seen kids in here is when their teachers bring a class, and even then they look like zombies. I head to the nonfiction stacks, my eyes scanning for my target. If I weren't in such a hurry, I might browse. I actually like libraries. Not this one, of course, but the fancy ones like New York Public on Forty-second Street, where everything is marble and wood — and free. Mrs. Resnick took our class there once when Mitzi and I were in elementary school. We went to hear story time, and then we ate hot pretzels on the big steps near the lions. I threw big chunks of mine to the pigeons. But what I most remember is all those little lamps on the tables and that scary quiet that let you hear our squeaky sneakers as we walked through the reading room, fingers to our lips. Mrs. Resnick whispered, "You can learn anything you want in a place like this."

We'll see.

"Can I help you?" The librarian's voice startles me. I turn around slowly and find a tiny, round lady looking at me over her glasses. She looks shocked to see a living, breathing person in here. Maybe she thinks I'm a spirit.

"Just browsing," I tell her, heading around the corner to the next set of stacks.

It doesn't take too much longer to find what I'm really looking for. It's on one of the top shelves in the reference section. It's the collection of school yearbooks, back all the way to the 1960s. I find the most recent volume, slip it under my arm, and head for the front desk.

"Sorry, that's noncirculating," the librarian tells me. Her hawk eyes are fixed on the words stamped on the inside cover: NOT FOR CHECKOUT.

My lightbulb goes on just in time, and I flash her my brightest smile.

"Oh, sorry. I'm new here. Mrs. Gregory in the guidance office sent me to borrow it," I say. "Just to see the clubs I might join. You have a library AV Club, don't you?"

I know: Genius.

"Seats, everyone! We have a lot of ground to cover." Ms. Shepherd rushes in with a pencil stuck behind her ear and a planner crammed with ungraded papers. As teachers go at DJ, she's good. She still decorates her room like we're little kids and brings snacks on Fridays. She calls us the "bright spot in her day."

I take my seat in the last row near the windows, far enough away from her to be safe. That's my favorite spot in all my classes these days, unlike Darlene, who likes to sit up front, where she can see in the teacher's grade book.

Ms. Shepherd scans the room. Today our *Julius Caesar* projects are due. Mitzi helped me sew my toga before she went home Sunday. We braided silk-and-plastic ivy into a wreath. "Who's first?"

I sink into my seat as Ms. Shepherd picks her first volunteer: (you guessed it) Darlene. She's written a sappy suicide note from Portia to Brutus and is doing a dramatic reading, complete with crocodile tears.

I hope Ms. Shepherd doesn't pick me to go today. Unfortunately, she calls on me all the time, and I can't seem to dodge her. Last week I didn't know what to write about for our descriptive essay. Finally, in desperation, I wrote about the crapping boxer from our old building. How it belongs to the Iraq War vet in 4C who looks like Jesus Christ. Ms. Shepherd made a big deal about it — writing long comments in the margins and reading out the part when the boxer gets to the stoop and sways on his old legs, with his nose in the air, like he's trying remember better days. I almost died. Not that I'm not glad she liked it. But couldn't she see my red face and know it was time to back off? Let's face it: standing out can only make a new kid public enemy number one. Then what? I'll be accused of being stuck-up *and* a suck-up. Better to blend into the herd. (Elephant wisdom never fails.)

I glance at the clock nervously, hoping she doesn't pick me, even though I know Brutus's speech by heart. I have more important things to worry about, namely, Yaqui Delgado.

Luckily, lots of other people volunteer, so I lay low and page through the yearbook in my lap as the drone of voices fades into the background. One presentation moves to the next, but I'm barely listening. A few kids have produced newspapers reporting Caesar's murder. Another kid made a diorama, although he could have used a little help from Mitzi and me. It's got LEGO people stuck in place with Play-Doh, and the crooked columns are made of packing Styrofoam. He's better at math, he explains. Not much of an art fan.

Darlene is outraged. Her sharp voice makes me look up.

"How can that [air quotes] 'project' even count for a grade?" she demands. "Anybody can stick dolls into clay. I did that in second grade!"

"We all have our artistic strengths, Darlene." Ms. Shepherd's smile always gets a little tight when Darlene comments. "Who's next? Anyone?"

Sally Ngyuen makes her way to the front of the

room. I'm about to start looking through the yearbook again when I notice something else for the first time.

SKANK is scribbled in ballpoint pen on my desk. I don't exactly know why my heart starts to thump. It's not like there aren't messages and other handiwork all over this school. Take auditorium seat J-8. I found out during last week's Expectations of Excellence assembly that it's got a faded image of a penis carved on the armrest. No one likes to sit in the Pecker Chair for an assembly. People make fun of you the whole day after that. Ask Rob.

Am I sitting in the Skank Chair, and I didn't even know it? Even when I cover the word with my binder, it feels like everyone knows, like the message was meant for me. That's what Yaqui called me, isn't it? Could she have spies in this very room? Could *she* be creeping on *me*? I glance around the room for suspects, but everyone has the same bored expression.

I open the yearbook and start paging through it as fast as I can. Basketball games, Ping-Pong, Yearbook Club, Drama. I check the cover to make sure it's not a mistake. It's like I'm reading about another place entirely. The school in this book has nothing to do with the place where I spend my days, the place where three in ten of us won't graduate. It doesn't show the empty air around me as I wait alone in the school yard, the bathrooms I won't go into, or the dead look I have to keep on my face as I go from class to class.

I turn pages furiously, running my finger down each row until I finally find her.

Yaquelin Moira Delgado. Moira? Quite a name, I note with satisfaction.

She's a thin girl with small eyes and hair pulled into a tight bun. She's staring right into the camera, her head tilted in a silly photographer's angle. Someone might call her pretty. I look closely, trying to memorize her grainy two-inch face. She sits at the lunch table with all the Latin kids. I remember her now.

I hate you, her eyes say.

"Earth to Piddy."

Ms. Shepherd is looking over her glasses, and the class is silent. She smiles with that hopeful look on her face, and I realize she's been calling my name. I slide the yearbook back inside my desk and sit up taller.

"Sorry."

It's no use. I'm busted. She glances at my lap from where she's standing midway up the aisle.

"What have you got there?"

My face is hot.

"Nothing."

She waits for a minute and walks closer, holding out her hand.

"It's just the yearbook," I say, handing it over. "I was just trying to . . ." My voice trails off.

Ms. Shepherd tucks the book under her arm. Everyone has shifted around to look at me, and my stomach starts to twist.

"Are you ready to present?" I can see she's saved me for last today, like dessert.

My hands feel heavy and wet. The clock says there are only seven minutes to the bell, almost time for the halls again, where Yaqui might be lurking.

"Piddy?" Ms. Shepherd asks. "Are you prepared?"

I keep my face blank as I push the bag with my costume farther beneath my desk. I don't know if it's stage fright or being in the Skank Chair or the fact that all at once Yaqui feels real. I open my mouth, but nothing comes out. I shake my head slowly as my fingers go to my necklace. The elephant goes back and forth, back and forth.

"I have a knife," a voice says from the other side of the room.

Ms. Shepherd whips around, momentarily terrified. Then she sees Rob standing up. He lifts his foil dagger out of the bag and shows her.

"Reynolds Wrap, I swear," he says. "I can go next. I'm ready."

Everyone laughs. At Rob? With him? I'm not sure.

"Very funny, Rob," Ms. Shepherd says, relieved. "Quiet down, everybody."

She turns back to me and writes something in her grade book as Rob makes his way to the front of the room.

34

"Come prepared tomorrow, or I'll have to make it a permanent zero," she whispers to me. "I don't want to do that, okay? It's killer on your average."

I stare straight ahead, trying to look like her disappointment doesn't bother me. The truth is I've never been given a zero. I've been second in line to Student of the Year since, I don't know, maybe third grade. (Mitzi always won.) Ma has all the honorable-mention certificates in a folder with her important papers.

This zero makes me feel weird, though. A little ashamed, sure, but also a little tough, especially with Darlene and the others looking on.

Soon Rob is stumbling over each line, murdering the soliloquy worse than Brutus did Caesar. He grips his dagger and jabs it hard in the air. If I didn't know better, I'd swear he was talking right to me.

"*O judgment! Thou art fled to brutish beasts. And men have lost their reason . . .*"

I grip my charm tighter. All I can think about is Yaqui Delgado's eyes, about what kind of cloak she wears, what kind of dagger she'll run through me.

CHAPTER 5

"Are you crazy? Crushing on *Alfredo*?" Darlene has me cornered at my locker. I can smell her Juicy Fruit gum. "Do you have a death wish or something?"

"Alfredo? What is it with this place and people I don't know?" I ask. "I'm not crushing on anybody."

That's a bold-faced lie. It's true that I have no idea who Alfredo is, but I do have a total crush on Mr. Grandusky, the student teacher in global history. He's got hipster glasses and a SAVE THE ELEPHANTS tie. When he asked me, "What defines something as a revolution?" I nearly fainted.

She crosses her arms. "Well, I heard you were talking to Alfredo in the school yard this morning. Just so you know, he's been Yaqui Delgado's boyfriend since, like, forever."

"I wasn't talking to *anyone* in the school yard." Then I think back to the two guys catcalling me. A sickening tug starts to work through my gut.

"You look guilty," she adds.

"No, I look annoyed." I slam my locker shut.

Darlene shakes her head.

"There's nothing to worry about, Darlene," I say firmly. "I've never even spoken to Alfredo. Now, let's go. We'll be late."

"What?" Mitzi shouts into the phone. "You have to speak louder! I'm in the gym."

She's at a badminton tournament, and I'm at the coin laundry down the street, trying to fill her in on my day.

What's wrong with this picture? Mitzi has always hated gym—until now. Unless I was the captain, she'd been picked last for every team except spelling bee since kindergarten. I should be happy for her, I guess, but I'm not. In fact, I'm irked. It's stupid to swing around those little rackets.

"You were right. It's a guy!" I shout.

"A lie?" she repeats.

"Never mind," I say. "Call me when you get home."

I hang up and stare miserably at the mesmerizing pinwheel of soapy clothes in the machine. Ma has picked up some more hours at Attronica, so now the laundry is on my plate, too.

"What? You have more important things to do?" Ma asked when I pointed out that I already make us dinner. "I'm making a living so we don't starve, Piedad. It's the least you could do."

Nobody is ever beating off starvation at Mitzi's house. Her parents are so utterly boring, old-fashioned, and ordinary. Her dad works at the clinic, and her mom volunteers, does the laundry, and cooks. Everybody does his or her job — and Mitzi's is only to study. I decide *that* annoys me, too. What would my life be like if my dad were still around? Easier, I bet, just like hers.

When I was little, I played a private game called Who's Papi? I could play it anywhere. The supermarket. The bus. Out on the street. I'd spot a man and imagine he was my dad in disguise, following me from a safe distance. I'd pretend he would introduce himself and say, "Piddy! I'm so sorry about everything. I've been thinking of you all these years." One day when we were back-to-school shopping, I almost followed a stranger into the men's room at a department store, pretending he was my father. "Where are you going?" Ma asked. She gave him a dirty look and ushered me away.

When the washer stops, I realize that my unhooked bras have hopelessly tangled in the laundry. One strap is so tight around the agitator that I have to climb halfway inside to get my stuff free. I've forgotten Ma's golden rule about hand-washing our personals. *Somehow she's always right,* I think, and that makes me feel even angrier.

The attendant looks up from her paper.

"Trouble, honey?"

"No. I'm fine," I grunt.

38

In the end, I don't try to pick it all apart. Instead, I shove the ball of clothes in the dryer and stuff extra quarters in the slot, hoping it will all dry anyway.

I open my history book and get to work. It's hopeless, even when I try to think of other things, like Mr. Grandusky asking, "What constitutes a revolution? Who's to blame for an uprising?"

I stare at the dryer and lose myself in thoughts that are just as circular.

What constitutes a crush? What constitutes talking to somebody? Who is to blame for my social failure?

CHAPTER 6

Two days later in the lunchroom, I learn a new game.

Yaqui Delgado teaches me.

It's called fastball, and you play it when none of the teachers are looking. This is a sport that is not included in our yearbook, but it is very real just the same.

Two teams: my lunch table vs. an enemy cloaked in invisibility. Equipment: a container of chocolate milk and a cinder-block wall. You don't have to ask to play or wait in humiliation as teams are chosen. In fact, if you're a loser, you're picked first.

Darlene is in the middle of complaining about our physics pop-quiz grades when an Elmhurst Dairy container comes whizzing through the air. It hits the wall right behind me and explodes like the big bang. Every genius at my table is doused in milk. For a second, no one moves. Rob looks as though he's crying chocolate tears. Darlene, dripping, stares at her hands through murky lenses. People around us start to point; a few that have been splattered at nearby tables curse on their way out the door.

I scan the blur of faces in the lunchroom, looking for the pitcher of today's fastball, but I already know exactly who it is. Most of the girls at the Latin table have their backs to us. All, that is, but one.

Yaqui.

I recognize her immediately thanks to her yearbook picture. She doesn't crack a smile as our eyes meet. She's sitting next to Alfredo. After she's stared me down, she turns back around slowly.

Meanwhile, Miss Posey, the lunch aide, comes running before I'm even on my feet. She's huffing with the effort of moving across the cafeteria so fast on her bunions. Chocolate milk is dripping down the walls, over the edges of the table, and onto the floor. She stares at the scene with disgust.

"Who threw it?" she demands, as though we're the guilty ones. None of us answers, too stunned to speak. "Custodian!" she barks into her walkie-talkie. "Custodian, do you copy?" She stops me from trying to get up. "Don't move. Any of you."

Inside, I'm flipping her the bird. Chocolate milk seeps through my shirt and jeans to my underwear.

The custodian rolls his bucket of murky water across the floor. His name is Jason, and he's young enough to still have acne on his neck. I try not to look at him as he works.

Not at him. Not at the guys all over the lunchroom who are pointing and cracking up. Milk drips from the ends of my hair. I'm a loser for all to see.

"Pick up your feet," he says.

I know what he thinks as he starts pushing his Pine-Sol mop in circles: we're easy targets. Weak. Weakness means that you deserve to be hated, that you deserve everything you get.

My fists are clenched; I want to punch someone. Rob is perfectly still, like his spirit has risen out of his body and nothing is left. Darlene rummages through her bag for her striped gym-suit top.

"My shirt is ruined," she fumes. "It was expensive, and now I'm going to *clash*."

I grab her arm before she storms off to the lockers.

"*What?*" she snaps.

My voice is almost a growl.

"I need to find out more about Yaqui Delgado."

Darlene rolls her eyes and cocks her head.

"Gee, ya *think?*"

CHAPTER 7

I walk home that afternoon in a daze. My shirt smells like baby vomit, and my hair has stiffened to peaks that I can't comb through. Chocolate milk is one of those things I remember loving as a kid. Now that memory's ruined.

"Hey."

When I look up, I'm surprised to find myself in front of the old building. My feet must have gone on auto-pilot. I'm like one of those African elephants that finds her way home, no matter how far she's roamed.

Joey Halper is sitting on the stoop, eating a frozen Popsicle, even though the October cold is biting through my jacket. He's grinning at me in that way of his. He has a new haircut — buzzed close to the scalp like a prisoner. He tries to look vicious, but it never really works. Even the day the cop car brought him home for shoplifting, he looked like a scared little kid to me. I'm pretty sure he was crying.

I never asked him about it, though. I don't ask Joey about a lot of things. And now his hair is so wispy that it looks like duck down, so soft you want to touch it. I know better, though. It's been a long time since Joey and I sat around catching caterpillars on the ends of twigs.

"Hey back," I tell him.

He squints, like it's an effort just to think about me, but at least he doesn't make any crack about my stained clothes.

"Didn't you move?" he asks.

"You noticed."

I can see the damaged staircase through the dingy glass. A plywood ramp covers the steps. Yellow CAUTION tape is pulled tightly all around, as if it's a murder scene. An unopened box of tiles is stacked in the corner.

"They still haven't fixed the steps?" I ask.

He shrugs.

"Who cares? But don't think I forgot that you owe me five bucks. I won the bet."

This makes us both smile. The day before the stairs went kaput, Joey and I had swayed on them like surfers.

"Five bucks says they don't last more than a week," he'd said as we rocked. It was like we were little again, back before Ma labeled him trouble and forbid me to cross the threshold to his apartment. I should have known that a kid like Joey could predict disaster better than I could. He has had a lot of practice watching for it. His dad drinks and drinks until his anger explodes. For Joey, timing a disaster is a science.

"So why are you back?" He chomps off a bit of Popsicle. "You miss me or something?"

My cheeks flush. He's cute for a future convict — even Mitzi used to think so — and the question catches me off-guard. Joey does that sometimes. Like the time he said, "What's worse? Having no dad or having a mean son of a bitch like mine?"

"Well?"

His question makes me feel especially silly in my chocolate-milk shirt. I think fast and point at the row of dented mailboxes inside.

"I came to pick up our mail and stuff."

He flashes a big smile. One of his front teeth has a tiny chip that I like.

"No way. People write to you, Toad?"

"Funny. Who writes to *you* besides your JD officer?"

"Ribbit," he says.

So much for a homecoming.

I step past him and press Lila's bell, but I can feel him watching me. Maybe it's my shaky ass at work again. I don't mind, though.

"Who is it?" Lila's voice is breaking up through the static.

"Piddy. Buzz me in," I say into the intercom. It feels weird not to live here anymore, not to have a key to unlock the lobby doors. I'm about to say so to Joey, the one kid I've known my whole life besides Mitzi, but when I look back through the glass doors, he's already gone.

The TV is blaring in Lila's apartment. She's a *novela* junkie, and *Los Diablos y el Amor* is her favorite. Three p.m., Monday through Friday, she's tuned in.

Lila blows on her wet nails and waves me in from the living room.

"Hurry up! You're just in time!" she says. "I think she's going to get her vision back today." On-screen, Yvette, our heroine, is in a hospital bed, her eyes bandaged. She's flanked by her husband — *and* her mother-in-law, who secretly engineered the accident a few episodes ago. There'll be hell to pay any minute, just the way Lila likes, with lots of yelling and threats. I drop my things and flop down on the sofa, not too close in case she gets a whiff of me. It feels good to be home.

Lila pushes a plate in my direction without a word. It's our usual afternoon snack: a sleeve of saltines and can of Goya Vienna sausages that Ma calls poison. I stuff my cheeks and slip off my spattered shoes. Heaven.

When the commercials come on, Lila turns to me.

"What do you think?"

She holds up her perfect almond-shaped nails. They're

46

painted black with a hint of red sparkles. "'Wicked'. It's new in the catalog this fall."

Cotton balls stained with her usual red polish are littered on the coffee table. The smell of acetone is a bad mix with sausages and sour milk. I try not to sit too close.

"New shipment?" I ask.

She plucks a cracker off my plate with the pads of her fingers and arches her brow as she takes a dainty bite.

"It arrived just this morning. And I should tell you that we're running a special, Miss Sanchez." Lila is using her businesswoman voice. She likes to practice on me before she wears down her good heels knocking on doors. "This polish is only $3.99. Regularly five dollars."

I try to picture vampy black-and-red nails on any of the tired-looking ladies on our block, but I realize Joey Halper would make a much better prospect. Black nails might look good with his do-it-yourself knuckle tattoos. Poor Lila. Ma's right. She's her own best customer.

"Hey, what happened to your shirt?" She scrunches up her nose at the stink. "And your pants?" There's a chocolate starburst pattern on my right thigh.

"Food fight in the cafeteria," I lie quickly. "What else have you got?"

"Have a look," she tells me, and turns back to the TV. "But don't steal all my samples like last time."

Her Avon case is open at her feet, and I'm happy to dig in. We've always called this case the Treasure Chest. Going through it makes me feel like I'm six again — in a good way. It's an old-fashioned model that looks bulletproof — black and hard on the outside. Lila could get a modern one, but this is the one she likes. She says it's the only way to keep all those pressed powders and glass bottles safe.

I pull out a small bottle shaped like a girl in a hoop skirt. She comes apart at the waist if you twist her hard enough. Her skirt is filled with a heavy jasmine splash. When she's drained, Lila will add her to the collection of bottles decorating her windowsills. Dried-out geishas, roses — breakable things of every kind that she can't bear to throw away.

The music swells on-screen, and I look up just in time to see that Yvette's bandages are being removed. Lila's eyes go wide in anticipation; she holds her breath, grabs my sticky knee. Even I can't help but stare at what's coming next.

The camera does a close-up on the girl who can miraculously see again. It cuts to the mother-in-law, then to the clueless husband. All at once, the credits run.

"¡*Maldito sea!*" Lila shoves the coffee table with her foot. "We have to wait to see that hussy get what's coming?"

"Please. You know what's coming." I rub perfume on my wrists and sniff. It's better than sour milk, and it reminds me of fancy department stores where I can only browse. I stuff a few samples in my pocket. "It's going to end the way all the *novelas* end. Everybody happy."

She shoos away my idea like it's a bad smell. "So what? Nobody gets happy the same way. That's what's interesting."

She glances at the clock with peacock feathers all around the rim and then gets a good look at me. I tuck my hair behind my ears, trying to look natural, but I'm a mess and she knows it.

"Mami working overtime again?" she asks.

I nod. There's a big sale this weekend, and extra shifts are the only way Ma could swing the move. She won't be home until nine tonight. I won't have to dodge her questions or make up stories about my clothes, but I'm in no hurry to sit over there all by myself, either.

"I can stay awhile. If you want."

Lila smiles. She always likes company.

"*¡Perfecto!* Then we have plenty of time."

"For what?"

"To pamper ourselves, of course." She leads me to the bathroom and drags in a chair. "You think I look this way without some work?"

In no time, my dirty clothes are in a pile, and I'm wrapped in one of her full body towels. She puts my head back, and soon the milk knots dissolve in the coconut shampoo. I close my eyes as she makes circles at my temples, just the way she does for her best customers at the salon. For the first time today, I almost relax and let my troubles wash away.

"You doing okay at that new school?" she asks after a while.

The whole awful day comes back behind my eyelids, searing me with shame. I hate lying to Lila, but I don't want to talk about it. I squeeze my eyes tight so no part of it escapes.

"Yes."

"But you haven't told me anything about it. That's not like you."

"You sound like Ma now," I say, annoyed.

"Ouch." Lila glances at my pile of soiled clothes and uses her soapy pinkie to flip on the radio she has perched on her hamper. It's tuned to La Mega FM. "How about some music, then, grouch?"

I don't say anything else as the sputtering radio fills the room. Lila wouldn't understand what it's like to be hated. Everyone loves her; everyone wants to talk to her at a party. Men dream about her. Women want to be her. I don't know that secret charm — at least not at DJ, where I've become a loser just like that.

Before I can help it, a tear slides from the corner of my eye and grazes my temple. I turn my head just in time to make it disappear in the water. Did she see? A shiver rises through my spine, but Lila doesn't say a word. She hums to the music like it's a lullaby and rinses me clean.

CHAPTER 8

Ma thought she'd be a piano teacher once. She studied all the way to the third-year examinations in Cuba, but once she got here to the States, there was no money for fancy lessons, much less any time to spend on hobbies. That's the only dream she's ever told me about, but she won't say too much else, since piano music reminds her of my father. Our piano is a relic from when my parents were together, so I don't know why Ma keeps it if she won't play it. Lila says Ma used to play a mean *tumbao*, but now she acts like the Steinway is just a place to prop up knickknacks. I'd love to be able to play some of those Latin grooves myself, but no matter how many times I've begged Ma to teach me, she says no. I even bought Latin sheet music and started teaching myself to tempt her, but she wouldn't bite. And it's hard to teach yourself to play the piano when you can barely read music.

"It's Bach you should listen to," she tells me every time I ask. "Not salsas by heroin addicts." Last year for

Christmas, she gave Lila a Kmart CD called *Timeless Masterpieces*, hoping to steer us both her way. I don't have the heart to tell her it's still shrink-wrapped in Lila's bookcase.

Sometimes I wonder if piano music is why Ma fell in love — or, as she says, "ruined her life." Not that she'd ever tell me. She keeps the story of her and my father to the CliffsNotes version: His name was Agustín Sanchez. He was from Santo Domingo, a real brain in his country, but he couldn't find work and came here. He played the organ every Sunday at Saint Michael's Church, the Spanish masses at eleven and two. He left before I was born. They were never married.

That's it. I don't even know what he looked like. There's not a single photograph left of him anywhere. Lila helped Ma burn every picture of him when he disappeared. Neither one of them is one bit sorry, either. Ma calls him "My Lousy Destiny." Lila just calls him "the Scuz."

In fact, all I have left of my father is his last name — and I think that's only because Ma couldn't stand the shame of leaving FATHER'S NAME blank on my birth certificate. What if the hospital people thought she was the kind of woman who couldn't remember the names of the men she slept with?

"Why do you want to know all that old history?" Lila says when I ask about him. "Your mother takes care of you, doesn't she? And I'm always here to help. Forget him."

"Because I want to know. What if I'm riding next to him on the bus and never even know it! What if he has other kids, and I marry my own brother by mistake and my kids come out funny?" I don't add the rest: *What if he's sorry and misses us and wants to send me to good schools and give me piano lessons?*

Lila shakes her head and looks at me with her eyes a little sad.

"Not a chance, *mija*. The Scuz went back to DR with his tail between his legs. Leave it at that."

I'm in my still nearly empty room again on Friday. I'm blasting an old *son* and dancing with an imaginary partner, waiting for Mitzi to call me back. I'm keeping a list of everything I want to tell her. She's been so busy these days. Practice. Tests. Clubs.

The phone rings, and I think it might be her. Unfortunately, it's Ma, and that ruins everything.

"Meet me at Met Foods at five."

It's four fifteen, and she's on break.

"We need some things, and I need your help carrying them," she says. "We got a big TV shipment today. My shoulders are numb."

"Can't we go tomorrow?" I beg. "I'll make us fried eggs and rice."

"Don't be lazy. Chicken is on sale, two for five. We'll take some to Lila. God knows if she's even feeding herself without us. You want her to end up looking like one of those scrawny Russian models?"

Ma hangs up.

By six thirty, I'm walking by the school yard with Ma. The sun is starting to sink behind the buildings, but unfortunately it's still daylight, so I can actually be seen. We're each hauling two bags; Ma's got the light ones with the plantain chips and napkins. I've got four roasters, which took Ma fifteen minutes to pick. She made me rummage through the whole refrigerator case to find the best ones.

The chain-link fence feels too long, especially with Ma's sneakers squeaking every step. She clutches her bag and frowns at the kids hanging out on the pavement, like she's ogling man-eating cats in a zoo. An old Pitbull song is blaring from a radio. The bass makes the ground shake. It takes everything I've got not to pump my hips and move to the beat.

I pray Ma won't start in. If there's one thing she can't pass up, it's warning me about life's dangers. They're lurking everywhere, from dirty toilet seats to strange men waiting in alleys for girls stupid enough to be out alone.

No luck.

"No one decent hangs out in a school yard, *oíste*?" she starts. She's loud enough to hear over the music.

"Shhh, Ma, please . . ."

"Look at that one." She actually points. "A savage on the street. *Qué chusma.*"

When I look across the yard, a jolt of fear runs through me. Of all people, it's Yaqui Delgado, live and in the flesh, like a nightmare that's stepped out into the real world. She's playing an old game called suicide with three other girls. I can tell she's lost the last of her points because she's leaning her back against the school-yard wall, waiting for the firing squad to shoot. The other girls start to launch their hard rubber balls, nine free shots in all, but Yaqui doesn't flinch. She keeps her hands behind her head and smiles, even when a ball hits loudly near her ears, even when one hits her squarely in the mouth. Those yearbook eyes are flashing with fire as she's pelted; it's like she wants more.

I keep my eyes down, hoping Yaqui is too preoccupied to spot us as we go by. Sometimes I swear Ma's going to get us killed with her mouth. I'm hurrying, but she won't let up. Decency is her favorite topic these days — or the lack of it. Working at Attronica only makes it worse. The news blares all day on dozens of screens until she's in knots. Rapes, attacks, beatings just for being in the wrong neighborhood. You name it. She's convinced the world has gone putrid. If I'm not careful, I'll be swept away in the tsunami of filth, too.

"*Son unas cualquieras,*" she mutters. Nobodies. No culture, no family life, illiterates, she means. The kind of people who make her cross to the other side of the street if she meets them in the dark on payday. They're her worst nightmare of what a Latin girl can become in the United States. Their big hoop earrings and plucked eyebrows, their dark lips painted like those stars in the old black-and-white movies, their tight T-shirts that show too much curve and invite boys' touches. The funny thing is, if I could be anything right now, I'd be just like one of them. I'd be so strong that I could stand without flinching if people pelted me with rubber balls. I'd be so fierce that people would cross to the other side of the street when they saw me coming. Yaqui and me, we should be two *hermanas*, a sisterhood of Latinas. We eat the same food. We talk the same way. We come from countries that are like rooms in one big house, but, instead, we're worlds apart.

From the corner of my eye, I see that Yaqui and a few girls have started to play handball now. It's a hard and quick game, all instinct. Yaqui's not wearing a jacket, even though you can see her breath in the air. A tank top shows off her cut shoulders. Me, I'm trailing my mother home with a bag of dead birds and frozen yucca, like a sap.

Ma sees me watching. "I didn't sacrifice to have you turn out like one of them," she says.

"Hurry," I say. The light up ahead is blinking yellow.

All I want is to get home. I don't want to hear about Ma's sacrifice right now. I've heard about *el bombo* a million times. Cubans couldn't come to the United States like people from other countries. They had to enter a freakish government-run lottery. That's what Ma did, and she likes to make it sound really dramatic. How she ran with her curlers still in her hair to mail her name to the lottery people. How she prayed to every saint for her name to be pulled for a visa so she could keep from starving. How when she first landed in America, she sat at the airport, waiting to be claimed like a piece of luggage by a cousin she'd never met. How she's worked like a dog ever since.

And so on.

I cut in front of a car just in time. Ma is older, slower, so she's stranded, waiting for the light.

"Piddy!" she shouts after me.

I'm sure Yaqui has heard. I don't slow down as my name echoes in the street. I'm practically running until I reach the door.

"What's the matter with you, Piedad?" Ma is out of breath when she finally catches up with me at the front door. Her sneakers have come unlaced, and she looks even more worn out than usual. She doesn't even try to say hello to Mrs. Boika, who is at her spot, guarding the last of the fading roses. "Where's the fire?"

I grit my teeth as I fumble for my key.

"How can you say bad things about someone you don't know?" I shout. "How can you hate a stranger? Why do you have to pick on people?" She's no better than Yaqui. It's like everywhere I look there's a bully in my face.

My key won't budge the sticky lock. I'm mute with fear and anger as I rattle the door and give it a hard kick. Ma blinks at me in surprise. The corner of her eye is jumpy as she straightens her back like a concert pianist on the bench.

"What's wrong?" she demands. "You're shaking. Tell me what's the matter."

What can I say that won't make things worse? If I tell her about Yaqui, she might storm to Daniel Jones in her squeaky shoes and rant to the principal about savages. Then I'm dead for sure.

"I hate this stupid apartment, okay? *I hate it.* I wish we'd never moved!"

Ma looks like she's going to say something else, but then she shakes her head and digs through her purse.

"*Dios de mi alma,*" she mutters. "You've been moody all week!"

It's been fifteen years since she's gone to Saint Michael's, but she crosses herself like a nun and shakes inside the blackness of her purse for her key.

CHAPTER 9

Saturday is the busiest day at Salón Corazón, and that's why Gloria Murí sometimes asks me to come in with Lila. I'm so bored on the weekends without Mitzi, and the tips are good. Besides, I need money to buy a new sweatshirt before the weather turns much colder. Turns out chocolate milk stains worse than blood.

Gloria is the owner, and business has been so good over the years that she's rich. She has a house in Great Neck and a lady who cleans and cooks for her. Everybody knows Salón Corazón. It's one part hair salon, three parts social hangout. She has six hairdressers, two shampoo girls, three manicurists, and me. As far as I know, there's only one golden rule she has for us employees — and it's not that you have to be legal, since she'll pay you cash if you want. No, what Gloria demands is that you make her clients happy. When she unlocks the door for business, she calls over her shoulder, "¡*Sonrisas!*" and that's our cue to paste on our happiest faces. She puts out endless pots of *café negro* and vanilla ladyfingers, and she never complains if her customers come a little late or hang around to talk after they're done. It's a beehive of gossip and harmless arguments shouted over the sound of the dryers. Sometimes it's so crowded in here, you can hardly move. You'd think it would drive her crazy, but no. This is just how she wants it.

"*Mijas*, in this business you have to be like an Alka-Seltzer!" Gloria always says. "A comforting relief."

Basically, my job is to fetch coffee, sweep up hair, and fold the hot towels from the dryer in the back. Sometimes, if there's a new nail-polish line, I'm the hand model, too, on account of my nice *uñas* that stay long. It's not bad except when Gloria's dog is in the shop — like today. Fabio is an old shih tzu with long hair. He's got one blind eye and a nasty disposition. If I'm not careful, he bites my ankles — hard. Not even my high-tops help against his needle teeth. I have to arm myself with a squirt bottle to keep him in line when Gloria's not looking. Nobody dreams of complaining to her about that nasty creature, though. She adores him; it's like she birthed him herself.

Gloria's next favorite is Lila, naturally. In fact, Lila's the favorite *champú* girl around here, making even more tips than the hairdressers. That's good news for me, since Lila sometimes takes me shopping on Saturdays, and she treats me to dinner, too.

As usual, she's been giving out love advice all morning—that, and inviting customers to her next Avon party, on Halloween night.

"I'll serve a little rum, play a little music, and make everyone have a good time," she says. "It will be a party!"

"I'll come if your boyfriend is the bartender," somebody calls out.

Lila laughs from deep inside as the room breaks into applause. Lately the hot topic everyone wants to know about is her boyfriend, Raúl the cop. I've met him a couple of times. He's all right. Big teeth, if you ask me. Who knows how long Lila will keep him.

"I saw you two dancing at the club," one of the manicurists says through her face mask. "He looks hotter than William Levy. Lucky!" She shakes her fingers like she's been burned. Giggles.

I just listen as I sweep. If you want to know anything about anybody's love life in Queens, come to Salón Corazón on a Saturday. You would not believe the private stuff a woman will say when she's in a plastic smock with a head full of foil. It's like the chemicals are a truth serum. In no time, she'll tell you all you want to know about her lousy husband and the good-looking neighbor with the big you-know-what.

Just then Fabio growls and lunges at my broom.

"Knock it off," I say, spritzing him. I didn't sleep well, and he's been nipping the whole morning. "¡Vete!"

"*¡Dios mio!* Is that Clara's girl?"

I look up from the pile of brown curls on the floor. A customer at Lila's sink is peering at me from under the towel she's using to guard her eyes. Uh-oh. It's Beba, the show-off cashier at Lewis Pharmacy. Her daughter, Merci, is studying medicine at Cornell on a full scholarship—which she has to mention in every conversation. Beba used to give me lollipops from behind the counter when I was little. She's a big lady with shelf boobs and full lips. If you didn't know better, you could take her for a guy in drag.

"Come here, let me take a look at you!"

Oh, boy.

"Yeah, that's Piddy." Lila winks at me as she works up a nice lather. "She'll be sixteen next week. Gorgeous, right? You should see her with her hair down."

I stand there feeling a little dumb. Any minute somebody's going to ask me if I have a boyfriend—or worse, how school's going.

"She looks just like Clara," Beba says. "*¡Igualita!*"

I glance at the mirror. Do I look *that* sour today? As sour as my mother? This is something I've never considered. My dark hair is pulled back in a ponytail, and I've broken out. I suppose she meant it as a compliment, though.

"*Gracias.*" I force a smile and go back to sweeping.

"Where do the years go?" Beba continues. "Just yesterday, my Merci was playing doctor with her dolls and *this* one was a sticky-fingered baby, and now look: Merci is studying at Cornell, and Piddy is all grown and beautiful." She turns to me. "Tell me the truth: I'll bet the boys die for you."

My cheeks feel hot. "Not really," I say.

But Beba isn't listening.

"Estás hecha una mujer." She shakes her head sadly. A lot of the salon women tell me this: "You've become a woman." None of them ever sounds too happy about it.

She pulls back her towel again and looks up at Lila as if something has just occurred to her.

"Now that we're talking about her, how *is* Clara, anyway? I haven't seen her in ages. Is she dating anyone?"

I almost laugh out loud. We're talking about Ma here, after all.

Lila shakes her head. "She says she's too busy."

"What woman is too busy for *un buen hombre*?"

Lila shakes her head again and sighs.

"I tell her, but she won't let me fix her up."

Beba clicks her tongue.

"Who can really blame her, though?" Her eyes cut to me and she finishes her sentence with a knowing look.

I stop pushing my broom. Ma dating is ridiculous. I can't even picture her enjoying herself here — with her friends. Ma hasn't set foot in Salón Corazón since I can remember — even though everyone else she knows comes here. She always says you can get just as good a haircut at the beauty school on Main Street for ten bucks, even though I know you're lucky to get out of there with both your ears still attached.

"*Mira para esto,*" Lila says, clicking her tongue. "Beba, how could you let your split ends go like this, *mija*? Your hair is spongy. I can't let you out of here looking like this." She motions to me. "Piddy, *por favor*, get me the deep conditioner from the back. It's in the red bottle with the pump top."

They're trying to get rid of me, of course. I move off but stop just inside the beaded curtain to listen. Luckily Beba's voice is big like the rest of her.

"*La pobre* Clara. I still remember that terrible day; don't you?" Beba says. "*¡Qué escándalo!* Agustín, that two-timer — he broke that woman's heart forever."

Fabio trots over and starts to snarl in the doorway. He curls back his lips to show his little razor teeth. His milky eye fixes on me.

"Shut up or I'll stuff you in the dryer," I hiss.

But it's too late. He erupts into a frenzy of yips and lunges. Lila turns around and peers around the doorway where I'm standing. She arches her brow.

"Piddy? Did you find it?"

I have no choice but to head to the supply room. It takes me a while to find the conditioner — way on the very top shelf next to the acrylic nail tips and wigged manne-quin heads, so Lila is already rinsing when I get back.

"What can I say, Beba? You know those types of men. They only know how to love with *this.*" She points to her groin. "Not with their hearts. And forget about loving kids . . ."

She spots me waiting by the beaded curtain and stops talking. I've been feeling sleepy all morning, but now I am suddenly very awake.

"Okay, Bebita," Lila says after I hand her the bottle. "Now let's see about this mane."

That evening we go shopping at City Fashion and stop for pizza at Vesuvio's. It's a dive, with a grimy floor and stuffing coming out of the vinyl seats, but it has the best Sicilian around. Lila lets long drips of orange grease slide onto her paper plate. I'm sitting in my new hooded sweatshirt, stirring my Coke with the straw and thinking.

"You're not hungry?" Lila looks at me carefully. My slice is untouched. "You've been so quiet and look a little pale. Maybe you're getting sick?"

"Did my father have another woman?" I ask suddenly.

The question hangs in the air for a few seconds like a bad smell.

"What?"

"Did my father fool around? I heard what Beba said about him breaking Ma's heart. Is that what happened?"

Lila drops her slice and wipes her puckered fingers.

"*Ave Maria,* Piddy. Do we have to talk about this stuff

65

when we're eating? You know my stomach. I'll have indigestion just thinking about that guy."

"Did he?"

She shakes pepper flakes all over her pizza in a fury.

"I don't want to talk about it."

"Just tell me already. It's not fair for Ma to keep something like that a secret, especially if other people know. How do you think that makes *me* feel?"

She puts down the shaker and sighs.

"Life's complicated, Piddy. People keep stuff private sometimes. Why should they go around remembering bad things? Besides, there's no rule that says you have to tell people everything in your past. Look at you. Are you going to tell me you don't have a few secrets of your own?"

She gives me a long look, waiting, but I don't answer.

"See?"

We eat in silence for a few minutes.

"Either he was a cheater or he wasn't," I say at last. "And I should know, either way."

"It doesn't matter," she says.

"It does." My throat squeezes into a stone as I say what I've thought for so long. "He left for a reason — because he had a girlfriend? Or because he just didn't want me?"

Lila stares at me a long time. Her long-last lipstick has finally worn off, and her face looks tired, even under her blush. Inside her brown eyes, I can almost see her torching all of my father's photos, bagging his ties and undershirts for the trash. Why all that rage and secrecy? Part of me doesn't want to know, the same part that wishes I could be a kid again and just let Lila hug me so I could feel her heartbeat through the wall of her chest. But I'm almost a woman now. That's what everyone says. There's no going back.

"Have you asked your mother?" she asks.

I shake my head. "You know Ma."

"Yeah." Lila stares at her chipped fingernail polish for a while. Then she whispers. "Your father took on a girl-friend, and he got caught. He didn't care who got hurt."

"He had a little *chusma*?" I ask.

Lila looks like she's going to be sick. Her lips are open-ing and closing as if she doesn't know what to say next.

"Come on, Lila," I say. "I'm nearly sixteen. When do I get to know the story of my own life?"

She takes a deep breath and nods.

"You should be talking to your mother about this, but I'm going to tell you because I love you. If you tell any-one I told you this — even Mitzi — I won't speak to you again. *Te lo júro.*" She makes the sign of the cross to tell me it's a sacred oath.

"Promise."

"Agustín was already married when he met your mother, Piddy. His girlfriend was your *mami*. Things got sticky when you came along."

For a second, I'm speechless. In fact, I'm sure I don't understand.

"Wait. You're telling me *Ma* had an affair? With a married man?"

She shakes her head, exasperated. "Look, let's forget this whole business. I shouldn't even be talking about this with you. Clara would tear the skin from my bones if she knew. I should never have opened my mouth."

But I don't stop.

"You're telling me that Ma got pregnant — by a married guy?" Then it all opens up to me. "Ma was a *chusma*?"

"Don't ever say that again," Lila says. "It was nothing like that." Her voice is loud and sharper than she's ever used with me. "She didn't have all the facts about the Scuz."

I stare at her in shock.

She takes a deep breath. "Sorry," she says. "It's just that you have to talk to your mother about this one, Piddy. Believe it or not, there are some things that even I know are not my business." She picks up her pizza and takes a savage bite. "Now, eat."

CHAPTER 10

The news leaves me in a daze around Ma. An affair with a married guy? It's hard to imagine her having sex before marriage — hell, even hard to imagine her having sex at all, really. It's like I don't know who she is. Or maybe I finally do. In any case, it explains so much about Agustín and why he's gone for good. For my whole life, he never remembered my birthday. I used to wonder what kind of dad doesn't remember his own kid's birthday. Come to find out, it's the kind who has a whole family someplace else, of course.

Not that I haven't had good birthdays. Real good, in fact. Take the year I was eight. Lila and Ma took Mitzi and me to the Bronx Zoo on the Q-44 bus. That's when I saw my first elephants and fell in love. They played with a ball on a rope. The zookeepers gave them a bath with push brooms and hoses, scrubbing their toenails and trunks. Afterward, Mitzi and I went in the gift shop, and Lila and

Ma let me pick out a present. It was my jade elephant on a thin silver chain.

"It means strength," the lady behind the counter said as she held it out to me. When we got home, Ma baked me a Duncan Hines cake and let me lick the bowl without any warnings about salmonella. We made a blanket tent on the sofa bed that night; Lila and Mitzi stayed over, too.

School is no better, though. Since the day I "played" fastball, when I step through the chain-link fence each morning, my shoulders hunch up, my mouth dries, and my head goes blank. A big cloud just swallows up everything about me. It's like the school yard is a big miasma — one of those make-believe poison clouds that scientists once thought killed you until they figured out it was actually microbes in water and microwaves and other stuff that really gets you. Yeah, DJ's a mind-erasing miasma, and it's eating my brain. I forget everything about velocity. I can't remember the reasons we were in World War I. Each period, I stare at the clock, thinking about getting from one class to the next without meeting Yaqui, like that's the real test. Sitting in class is just what I do in between.

Darlene and I are on our way to math, and she's complaining about Mr. Nocera's rumored pop quiz when someone smacks the back of my head. It happens so fast that at first I think it's an accident. That's how stupid I am.

I don't even know I'm in big trouble until it has swallowed me whole.

Darlene stares straight ahead and starts walking fast.

Another whack, this time harder.

I whip around and find two girls I don't know. They're pretending they didn't touch me, but they're cracking up, and it's obvious that I'm the punch line.

"Quit it," I say.

"Quit what?" one of them says.

Suddenly there's a tug on my neck from behind, and with a tiny *pop*, I feel the spidery links of my chain break apart. I grab for my neck, but it's too late. When I look, I see Yaqui walking away through the crowd.

"Hey!" I shout as I try to follow. The girls block my way, and soon the wall of bodies in the halls is thick. I try to push through, but people push back, annoyed. Through the spaces between shoulders and backpacks, I think I can still see Yaqui, the small bun at the back of her head.

"Give it back!"

A few kids turn to look, but by the time I squeeze through them, Yaqui and her friends are gone again. All I see are colors, shirts, and ugly faces.

The bell rings, but as the hall empties, I still can't move. I stand there, trying to decide what to do. I've been mugged at school, but even Darlene has vanished and left me alone. I don't blame her, really. I've started to cross over to the place where I'm too dangerous to know. My trouble might be contagious, and no one wants to catch this social disease. I get on my hands and knees and search every inch of the hall, up and down both sets of staircases. I rub dust bunnies in my fingertips, trying to find my elephant among the chewed pen caps and broken hair bands.

Nothing.

My dirty hands are still shaking when I finally get to class. My face feels hot, but my neck is unnaturally cold. Nothing feels real to me. Everyone stops and looks up from their quiz as I stand stupidly in the doorway.

"Tardy," Mr. Nocera says.

"But I lost something," I say.

"You certainly did: ten minutes to work on your quiz."

"Something important," I insist.

"Check the lost-and-found during lunch." He's already scribbling in his attendance book. "Two latenesses make a detention, Miss Sanchez. I run a tight ship."

I look right through him and head to my seat, fuming. Darlene puts her foot out to stop me as I go down the aisle.

"You're not going to tell, are you?" she whispers. "If you are, leave me out of it, for God's sake. I *don't* want to be a witness."

Now it's my turn to roll my eyes.

"Get out of the way." I push past and slide into my seat. How stupid does she think I am?

My head is starting to pound. I'm too mad to take the quiz Mr. Nocera hands me. Instead, I put my head down and stare out the grates until I don't see the bars of this cage anymore. There's only one thing I know for sure: I have to get my necklace back. The question is: How?

CHAPTER 11

The guidance office is in room 109, along the only sunny stretch of hall in this whole stupid school.

I watch through the glass of the office door, where Darlene is on the phone, looking like the thirty-year-old she'd like to be. She's a student aide there, getting credit instead of taking a study hall, which she refers to as a "waste of learning time." Naturally, all the secretaries adore her. When she's wearing the volunteer badge, she's responsible, a little snippy, and has a good phone manner. A Mini-Me of their very own.

It has taken some convincing to corrupt her. I had to swear I'd never use her as a witness, no matter what. Also that I'd help her with physics homework for the rest of the year.

I pretend the bulletin board in the hall is interesting as I wait for her to get what I need. Our crime is taking even longer than I thought; I should already be in study hall, and any minute one of the wandering teachers on duty is going to find me and shake me down for a pass. It's not like I can hide in the bathroom. Who knows what would happen if Yaqui's crew found me in there?

The board is crammed with posters. Registering for the draft. College visits. SAT dates and codes. A science academy for juniors and seniors at the community college. One poster catches my eye. It has a bulldog inside a circle with a diagonal red line. BULLY-FREE ZONE. STAND UP. SPEAK OUT, it says. I almost laugh out loud.

"Here," Darlene whispers, peeking out the door a few minutes later. "Yaqui Delgado's schedule." It's tucked under an application for the science academy. She tugs at her skirt nervously as I look the paper over. "I hope you know I could get in real trouble for this. Accessing student records is, like, *illegal* for an aide."

"You're a secret badass, though," I say to make her feel better. "Thanks."

I look at the home address and try to place the street. If I'm right, it's in the Bland — a shit hole if ever there was one. Figures. I scan the schedule for room numbers and classes. Yaqui and I don't share a single teacher or classroom in this school, and yet I can't get away from her. How does that happen? I fold the sheet carefully and slip it inside my backpack.

"You're welcome," Darlene calls.

I hurry down the hall.

There are two little rectangles of glass on the classroom door, both covered with black construction paper. Through a space at the edge, I look inside. According to her schedule, Yaqui has health this period.

I'm almost giddy standing there. My head is starting to thud at the temples, a faint beat getting louder by the second until at last I recognize what's sneaking out through my brain. It's the steady *clave* of a salsa, a classic two-three beat. *Pa-pa/pa-pa-pa/Pa-pa/pa-pa-pa.* The band in my aching head is waiting to play so Yaqui and I can go *mano a mano* in our dance.

What am I going to do, now that I'm standing here? What do I tell the teacher? That I need to talk to Yaqui Delgado? And if I do get to talk to Yaqui, it will be to say what, exactly? *Give it back, you thief?* The whole plan suddenly seems stupid.

"Where are you supposed to be?"

Ms. Shepherd has come out of nowhere, and when I turn around, I find her pointing at me with the antenna of her walkie-talkie. She's on hall duty, looking for skippers like me, and she's even wearing sneakers for the occasion. It occurs to me now that I've never skipped before. Ms. Shepherd looks surprised when she sees me at first, then just disappointed.

"Piddy?"

I don't answer, but not because I'm being rude. It's as

if she's talking to someone else. I don't feel anything like the kid Ms. Shepherd hoped for a few weeks ago. The fact is I'm losing my shine in her eyes, the same way I'm losing it for Mr. Nocera and all my other teachers. I didn't turn in my English homework yesterday, another dent in my shiny armor. Somehow, I couldn't find the energy to care about participial phrases.

"What are you doing out of class?" she asks.

My head is swirling, and it feels as if she is talking to me from far away.

"Are you all right? You look sick."

"I thought I had health, but I made a mistake," I lie.

She puts her finger on the walkie-talkie's button and taps the antenna to her lips. She could check my schedule in a second and bust me right here. "The bell rang six minutes ago."

"I had to stop in guidance first. To pick up magnet-school stuff." I hold up the stapled application to show her.

She nods, thinking.

"Piddy, I've been wanting to talk to you about your work in English."

Before she has a chance to say more, I take a step back.

"I'll do better," I mumble, losing my nerve completely. "I should get to study hall."

The beat in my head is threatening to split my skull wide open. I make my way down the hall, but when I get to the stairwell, my eyes become glued to the exit door. I don't have the courage to face Yaqui, and now I can't breathe in this school. I can't see who I am or hear my own voice. I'm already late, and who cares if I'm marked absent and unexcused from study hall? I reach for the side doors and push myself into the quiet world outside. The cold sunshine is blinding.

I don't go home. Instead, I walk two blocks to the bus stop and climb on the next bus to kill time. This one is headed toward the subway, but in the middle of the day, it's nearly empty. I settle in at the back.

She stole my elephant necklace. I type the message to Mitzi into my phone and wait for her reply as I ride. Ten whole minutes go by and nothing.

I stare out the window, brooding and feeling ignored. The bus skirts the projects where Yaqui lives. Tall buildings and tagged benches with guys just waiting for nothing. I look high up as we go by, trying to imagine from which ugly window Yaqui looks out onto the world.

Up at the front of the bus, a man signals for a stop. He's about Ma's age, tall with salt-and-pepper hair. A folded newspaper is tucked under his arm. I can't help it; I start to play my old game. He likes *plátanos fritos* and cheeseburgers like me, I decide. He likes nature shows. By the time he's climbed down to the sidewalk, I can almost imagine his voice deep and calm in my ear as he tucks me into bed.

"Piddy, I'm so sorry for everything. I've thought of you all these years. Don't worry. I'll keep you safe. And here, I've written a song just for you."

I ride to the bitter end of the line, thinking of my imaginary father and humming his made-up tune.

CHAPTER 12

"You're not doing your work?"

Ma's voice is tight as she sits down at the kitchen table while I'm trying to do my homework. The fried steak and white rice I made for her is still wrapped on the stove. She hasn't touched it.

Instead, she's staring at the progress report from Daniel Jones that arrived in today's mail. Had I known that DJ mails home interim reports, I would have watched the mailbox more carefully, maybe bombed it with firecrackers or set it on fire the way Joey does to his. Now Ma's mad, and she's asking questions. She rubs her shoulders and frowns as she reads in her heavy accent.

"The student is inattentive. The student has missed assignments."

"Ma—"

"The student is not working up to his or her potential."

She puts down the page and gives me a disgusted look. Then she counts the row of zeroes on the computer print-out with her pinkie.

"It says here you have six zeroes. *Seis.*"

I don't answer. My head still hurts, and Ma's voice makes my shame worse.

"Well?"

"It's a hard school," I explain. Hard to survive. Hard to be left alone. I stare at my math book and try to look busy. I haven't paid attention in class all week, and now I have no idea how to apply this stupid theorem. I read the directions over and over, but nothing penetrates. Ma doesn't make it any easier with her eyes boring into me.

"A zero doesn't mean something is hard, *niña,*" she says. "It means you're lazy. It means you're not studying. *Nada. !Qué vergüenza!*"

Ma sits down across from me. "You should be ashamed. You used to be an excellent student. Now this. Do you want to end up a little lowlife? Eh? ¿*Una chusma?* Look at you! You're practically playing the part."

She points to my new T-shirt that I got when I went shopping with Lila. It's a little tighter than I usually wear, and it has a V-neck. Lila said it showed off my figure.

"I bought it with my own money," I point out. "I can't dress like a ten-year-old my whole life."

Ma sighs. "So what if it's your money? A shirt like that

sends a message, *oíste*? What? You want people to think you're no good like your father?"

"I wouldn't know about my father, would I?" I mumble.

"Eh?"

"I said, 'I wouldn't know.'" I reach for my necklace to comfort myself, but of course it's not there. It's like a phantom limb on a soldier. Bile rises into my mouth. I feel sick. Why can't she leave me alone?

"What do you mean?" she says.

Ma scoops out some Iodex and rubs the ointment into her neck as she waits for my answer. Her Attronica name tag is pinned on crooked, and there are sweat stains under her arms. For a second, I can see her the way her boss does at the warehouse: just another nobody loading boxes, and I hate her for it.

I grip my pencil until I feel like it might snap.

"It means you don't bother to tell me anything about my father, Ma. How would I know what he was like? I don't even know what he looks like thanks to you. I have to hear about my own life from other people at a friggin' hair salon."

She stops rubbing and gives me a careful look.

"Oh? And who has been talking about us at the salon?"

"Forget it."

She wipes her hands clean, shaking her head in disgust. "That place is like a radio station, you know. It broadcasts everything." She crosses her arms. "So, what is it, then? Somebody is spreading gossip about me and Agustín?"

I ignore her.

"What have you heard?" she asks louder. Her oily hand covers up the words on the page and makes a mentholated stain on the problem I'm trying to work out. "*¡Contéstame!*"

I snatch the book away and glare.

"Do you want me to do my homework, or do you want to bother me all night? Jesus, Ma, you're such a pain! I can't stand you!"

The minute I say it, Ma flinches, and I wish I could eat my ugly words. I've never been so mean to her, but now all I want is to make her feel small. I need her company down here at the bottom of this pit, where maybe she can hug me and tell me it's all right. But she's made of sturdier stuff. She doesn't fall after me the way I want. Instead, she sits back and arches her brow.

She lets out a deep laugh, shaking her head, as if I'm the stupidest little kid she knows. Then she folds the progress report carefully, her hands barely trembling as she leans in.

"You know what, Piedad Maria Sanchez? This has nothing to do with Agustín. It has to do with you. You're going to do better in school, you hear me? You're going to do better, or I'm going to go down and see what's so hard for you at that new school. Understand? I didn't sacrifice—"

I slam my book shut and head for the door. It's dark outside, and it's me who's shaking now.

"Where are you going all alone? It's dark," she says.

"Away from you!" I shout.

I ring and ring at the lobby doors, but Lila is not home. The apartment looks dark from the street. She is probably out dancing with her William Levy look-alike. The whole idea makes me even angrier. Worse yet, I didn't grab a coat, and now I'm shivering under my sweatshirt. I rattle the door to see if someone might have left it loose, but it's locked tight.

I'm just about to turn back for home when somebody opens an apartment door inside. It's Joey Halper. He's holding his boots in his hands and his army jacket over his shoulder. He looks surprised to see me. Then he stops on the other side of the glass door, cocks his head, and smiles.

"Trying to get in, Toad?" he asks.

"Open up."

"You have to tell me the secret password."

"Is it 'Shut-up-and-open-the-door-Joey'?"

He snorts and shoves his bare feet into his unlaced work boots. Then he opens the door.

"She ain't home," he says as I start to storm past him. He knows exactly who I'm looking for, of course. From the hall, I can hear the canned laughter of the show his father is watching on TV. Joey walks out to the stoop and looks up at the sky as he puts on his coat. The stars are already peeking out. "Come on," he says.

The cellar door is around the back of the building, right next to the super's apartment. The basement has always been creepy, and not just because of the super. It has cracked cement floors and those little windows that only show you people's feet as they go by. When we were little and bored, Joey and I would play hide-and-seek all over the building, but this was the only place I wouldn't come to find him, even if I knew for sure that he was here. The super had a rule against kids playing in the basement, and I was scared he'd shut me in that cold, dark place forever if he caught me playing there. That feeling never went away. Even when I got old enough to know better, the padlocked door at the far end always scared me. It led to the storage units for each floor, but you could probably hide a body in there and nobody would ever be the wiser.

Joey unlocks the door and lets us in. My teeth are practically chattering from the cold, so he fishes in his pocket for a few quarters and turns on the old dryer. In a few minutes, it gives off heat and a musty odor laced with a touch of bleach. It's strangely comforting as I press my hands on the sides to warm them. He climbs on top of the dryer as if it's a chair and gnaws on his cuticles, waiting for me to warm up. Little white puffs of his breath explode from his lips with each pull. One of his wrists is swollen with new ink, I notice. It says: HOMEMADE PAIN.

"Doesn't that hurt?" I ask. Last summer, he showed me his tattoo tools: a cigarette lighter, a sewing needle attached like a harpoon to the eraser end of a number-two pencil, and a jar of India ink he swiped from the art room.

He shakes his head.

"I take it like a man."

"Sure," I say.

"I'm going get a good one when I'm eighteen. A cobra right here." He lifts his shirt to show me his hip. His jeans sit just under his navy-blue boxers. The skin on his stomach is smooth and tight, and the slope of his hip bone disappears inside his pants in a way that makes me blush.

Suddenly Joey hops down from the dryer and heads for the storage area. In no time, a dim light is switched on, and I can see one of the rusty doors is hanging open. He's gone for a long time.

"Joey?"

No answer.

I know I should go home. I should say sorry to Ma. Still, one foot moves in front of the other until I reach the doorway. The ammonia smell that greets me is overpowering.

A bare bulb swings from a chain on the ceiling. There's an artificial Christmas tree in one corner and stacked boxes. Joey is sitting on a striped mattress on the floor. He doesn't look up when I step inside. Instead, he keeps staring at something in the corner. That's when I see an old laundry basket lined with a towel. Inside is the mother tabby suckling two kittens. It's not ammonia I smell. It's cat piss. My heart gives a jump. They're only palm-size, and they're just fluff with big heads and eyes still closed to the world. They can't be more than two weeks old. As they nurse, they jerk their paws and heads in blind clumsiness; the orange one even rolls off its mother's teat helplessly. Joey gets up and picks the kitten up carefully, putting it back near the basket as the mother hisses.

"Shut it," he tells her.

"Oh, my God," I say, getting next to him on the mattress. "Where did you find them?"

"Last week, behind the dryer," he whispers. "I put them in here and feed them, but I let the mother out at night to hunt so she doesn't get bored."

"Aren't you scared the super's going to catch you?"

Joey smiles. "I'm not afraid of anything."

Neither one of us speaks for a long time as we watch. After a while, he lies back with his hands folded behind his head. I try not to look at him lying down that way, even though I can feel him staring.

"You glad you moved, Toad?" he asks finally.

From here, it's as if his eyes are glowing like a cat's. For once, he isn't wearing one of those grins. He looks just the way he did when we were ten, soft and open. I look down at him and shake my head slowly.

"No. It's horrible."

Joey takes his jacket off and puts it around my shoulders. Then he presses me back gently until he's on top of me, and his lips are brushing mine. His body feels warm in a way that I need. He cups my face with his tattooed hands, and when I close my eyes, he kisses me.

The super's TV is a hum in the background as Joey explores my mouth. Over the dryer, I can also hear the angry rise and fall of Mr. Halper's voice, surely the start of another argument, but Joey doesn't seem to pay attention to the sound of chairs being dragged, maybe tossed over. Joey runs his lips along my bare neck and nuzzles me like one of the kittens as I take in the smell of his dirty hair. He moves his hands over my bottom until I'm twitchy with need. I don't know how long we lie there kissing, but when he finally starts to slide his chilly hands inside the back of my pants, I push him and sit up, afraid. My mouth is still tingling; I'm dizzy.

The dryer has stopped, and the cellar is silent and cold as a tomb. I slide off his jacket, but he doesn't reach for it. Joey turns on his side and stares at the sleeping kittens as I head for the basement door.

"I have to go," I mumble.

Joey doesn't say good-bye.

CHAPTER 13

"I'm sick, Ma."

Lying here in bed, I feel broken into a million pieces. My head is a brick, and my legs don't want to take me to school. I hold the covers around my chin as Ma frowns and feels my forehead. I can still feel Yaqui's friends smacking the back of my head.

"That's what happens when you go out at night, *desabrigada* with no coat," she says. "It's a miracle you didn't get pneumonia."

I don't say anything. Who wants to fight again?

According to her palm, I might have a small fever. Ma hurries off to the kitchen and comes back with a cup of tea, aspirin, and a jar of Vicks VapoRub that she sets on the floor by my bed. I'm too old for her to take a sick day for me. Besides, she never takes a day off unless it's an emergency — like when I had to have my appendix out. And now it's getting close to the holidays, and the back room at Attronica is becoming a maze of boxes, floor to ceiling, in preparation for the season.

"I'll call you at lunch. Stay in bed." She pulls on a jacket. "Lila's home if you need something," she adds before she heads out the door.

Relief washes over me as she leaves for the bus stop. Staying home means Yaqui doesn't have to exist today. I don't have to disappoint my teachers. I don't have worry about my shaky ass or anything at all today. I close my eyes and turn over, nestling deep inside my covers for a rest, when I hear the bus pull away from the curb. I'm already drifting off.

I am beautiful, riding on the neck of a huge, jeweled elephant. She's massive and graceful, and her skin is the mottled green of jade. She trumpets and flaps her ears to warn onlookers to stay back. I can feel people's fear and respect as we go by. They marvel at my long hair, which trails down my back, at my legs, my balance, my total control.

I ride down Parsons Boulevard; there are no cars. No one bothers me out here. Crowds stare and applaud. Joey Halper calls out my name. Agustín Sanchez plays a piano on the rooftop just for me. He hits a high C on the keyboard again, and again, and again . . .

Someone is leaning on the doorbell.

My clock says eleven thirty; I've been asleep for

three hours. I crawl across my bed to the window and peek out through the blinds. Lila is staring at me from below. When she spots me, she waves a white paper bag above her head.

"Let me in!" Her voice is muffled through the glass. "I'm freezing to death!"

I wrap the comforter around me and ring her in. A minute later, Lila steps into the apartment, shivering.

"*Cristo*, it feels like December out there." She hands me a greasy Dunkin' Donuts bag. "Lunch: special delivery."

Inside is a Boston cream doughnut, my favorite.

"Oh, I love you."

"Didn't you hear me ringing? I was about to knock on the old lady's door to let me in." She tosses her jacket on the coatrack and rubs her hands together to warm them. I can see her new nail polish, a navy blue.

"I fell asleep," I say. "And, anyway, Mrs. Boika wouldn't have let you in. I don't know what her problem is. She hasn't said two words to us since we moved here."

"Racist old bat," Lila mutters, and starts for the kitchen, where I settle in at the table, the bulky comforter around me like a cocoon. When I sink my teeth into the doughnut, cream squirts down my chin. Lila makes a face.

"Don't judge me," I tell her, licking my fingers. "I'm starved." My hair is coming out of my ponytail, and my lips are parched and cracked.

She puts the *cafetera* on the burner, opens Ma's catchall drawer, and pulls out a hairbrush.

"At least let me make you presentable. I'll comb you out."

She stands behind me and lowers the comforter as I take another bite of doughnut. Suddenly she sucks in her breath.

"*¿Y esto?*"

"What?"

She taps the back of my neck with the brush, and I reach for the spot. Is it zits on my back again? Chicken pox?

"You got a nice hickey, *mija.*"

"*What?*" I run to the bathroom mirror to check. Sure enough, when I crane my neck, the edges of a dark raspberry are showing. The sight of it makes my heart race. Suddenly I remember Joey at my neck. Now I want to see him again — just to rip off his stupid lips.

"Shit, shit, *shit.*" I hold a hand mirror and turn around to see the full damage. It's huge and purple as a bruise. The guy has lips like a bass.

Lila follows and leans against the doorway, amused.

"So, who is the little sucker?"

My face goes a deeper red than the hickey.

"Nobody."

"Really?" she says, laughing. "You gave yourself a *chupón* on the neck? Nice trick. You should join the circus!"

I scowl at her and start to yank my hair out of the matted ponytail. Maybe my hair can hide this until it fades. Tears spring to my eyes as I rip strands from the band.

Already, I'm making a mental list of all the turtlenecks I own. Only two. Jesus! I've got to get to the store. If Ma spots this, I'm dead.

Lila reaches for my hand to stop me.

"Calm down, already. You don't want a bald patch, too, do you?"

"What am I going to do?"

"Wait here." She disappears and comes back holding a sample tube of foundation. "Try this. If it can hide the circles under my eyes, it can hide anything."

She doesn't say a word as I glob the tan liquid on the spot. A few minutes later, the hickey is barely there. It's nothing more than a secret.

When I'm done, Lila steps inside the bathroom and kisses my cheek. She brushes my dirty hair in long strokes until it's smooth and covering my neck.

"It looks nice down," she says softly. "It makes you look grown." She moves her pinkies gently over my full brows and runs her palms over the slope of my cheekbones as she studies my reflection in the mirror.

"What?" I say.

"Your mother is worried about you, Piddy."

Great. They've been talking.

"Ma is always worried."

"True. But should she be this time? She said you disappeared last night. She didn't know where you went. That's not too safe."

I don't answer.

She puts her face next to mine as she admires me in the mirror. I can smell the perfume she always dabs behind her ears, until the smell of espresso coming from the small pot on the stove overpowers it.

"Just be careful about letting boys touch you, Piddy. It feels good, but it's not a game, no matter how much fun you think you're having."

I look at her carefully. Fun? Was I having fun with Joey?

"Is that what you think when you're with Raúl?"

Lila doesn't blink. It's a fair question, and she knows it.

"No," she says. "But I should."

The phone rings as Lila is draining her mug. The caller ID says DANIEL JONES HIGH SCHOOL. I answer it.

"Is this the parent or guardian of Piedad Sanchez?" The voice on the other line is strangely familiar.

"Yes," I say.

The caller snorts. "Oh, *please*. It is *not*."

"*Eh kyoos me?*" I say, trying to imitate Ma's accent.

"Quit it, Piddy. It's me: Darlene."

"Oh." I let out my breath. Making attendance calls must be one of her aide duties. I can hear phones and voices in the background. "You scared me for a second. What do you want?"

She turns on her secretary voice.

"I'm verifying your illness today."

"I'm sick, Darlene. My mother knows."

Darlene lowers her voice.

"Well, who cares about that?" It sounds as if she has her hand wrapped around the receiver. "Of all days to be absent, Piddy! You missed it all. You won't believe it."

"Believe what?"

"She got busted!" she says.

"Who?"

"Are you kidding me? *Who?* Yaqui Delgado, that's who! The cops came with dogs and everything."

My mouth hangs open.

"Is this a joke, Darlene?"

"Dead serious. I'll tell you everything tomorrow. Gotta go," she says. "Oh, and bring an excused note, or I'll have to write you up."

The phone goes dead.

CHAPTER 14

I've heard the ladies at Salón Corazón say that miracles happen every day. You wake up to find your garden statue of *la Virgen* crying tears. Your uncle's bad tumor dissolves overnight like a sugar cube. Once one of the manicurists even found a hundred bucks in her smock pocket on rent day, though Gloria swore she didn't put it there.

I always thought they were lying, but now I get this early birthday present from God, and what can I say? It's like *el Señor* himself put his hand out to help me in my time of need.

Darlene is waiting for me in the school yard when I get there the next day. She fills me in on the good news. Yaqui Delgado was suspended.

"The po-po hauled her off." Darlene is practically hopping up and down like a third-grader — not exactly gangsta. "They caught her stealing somebody's cell phone right out of their backpack in the hall yesterday. I was subbing in the front office while they were writing her up. That's, like, larceny. You had to see it. She told the cop to eff himself."

"Did her parents show up?" If I stole something, Ma would be a much worse fate than any cop. Besides, I've been wondering what kind of people spawn a Yaqui. It's not every day you get Hate on Two Feet.

"Just a caseworker. Big surprise." She rolls her eyes. "Anyway, I'll bet that's a level-four offense — an automatic three days out of school — or at least in-school suspension for a week! Who knows? Maybe she'll get jail time, and she'll rot in prison! You never know."

I can't believe my ears, but Darlene's smile tells me God's miracle is true. I'm going to light our Virgin candle when I get home.

The bell rings, and the herd of kids starts up the stairs. I wonder if the cops will give back the stuff Yaqui took. Will I get my jade elephant back again, after all? I let out a breath and imagine Yaqui lying helpless on a jail floor, rats in her hair. It's going to be a great day.

Ma used to try to make me feel better about things by pointing out people who were worse off than we were. Back when I used the free-lunch form, she'd tell me about all those kids in the Third World starving and getting worms through their bare feet. I suppose she thought that would make me feel better about having to turn in that form in my old shoes, right there in front of everybody's prying eyes.

"You could be one of those hungry kids," she'd tell me as she forced the paperwork into my hand. "Be grateful you're not."

That's what comes to mind when I get to my locker. I'm unpacking, still a little drugged from the joy of a Yaqui-free school day, when I notice that there is a new word written on Rob's locker. HOMO, it says. The go-to insult when "loser" isn't quite enough.

Jesus. Where's the Bully-Free Zone now?

Maybe it's all the light-headedness over my Yaqui-free day ahead that gives me courage. But just like that, I uncap my Sharpie and get busy covering the letters with thick squiggles. I've had some good luck today. Why not pass it on?

I'm practically done when someone suddenly taps me.

"What do you think you're doing?"

It's Coach Malone. He sniffs at the strong scent of marker and gives me a nasty look.

"It had a bad word." Instantly, I feel like a liar, even though it's true. There's no proof left. You can't see a trace of anything under my handiwork.

He whips out his pad and pen.

"Name."

Mr. Flatwell, dean of student discipline, is not a friendly man. According to his framed diplomas, he's actually a graduate of John Jay College of Criminal Justice, a pretty screwed-up springboard for a high-school educator, if you ask me. He's tall and dark, with buzzed hair. He's wearing a clip-on tie, I notice, in case someone tries to choke him, I guess. His muscles show through his shirt. Nothing decorates his desk but a computer, stack of passes, and a walkie-talkie that keeps clicking and sputtering, even with the volume turned down low. He has my school record pulled up on his computer screen, and his burly hands are folded.

"Pee-ay-dad Sanchez," he says, scanning the referral. "Let's see what brings you in for a visit this morning." When he finishes, he looks up at me coolly. "Defacing school property."

"That's not true." I pull nervously on my turtleneck. This office is hot, or maybe it's my nerves.

"Really? Coach Malone lied?"

Uh-oh. A trap.

"That's not what I mean," I say. "The locker was already messed up. I was trying to fix it."

His eyebrows shoot up.

"With a permanent black marker?" He leans back and pulls out my confiscated Sharpie from his shirt pocket. Exhibit A. Contraband per the student handbook.

The whole thing sounds stupid, even to me.

"Somebody wrote an ugly word on the locker," I explain. "I wanted to get rid of it."

"I see. What did they write on your locker?"

"It wasn't on my locker. It was somebody else's."

"Okay: somebody else's locker. What did it say?"

I try to size him up. You never know who you're talking to. He could be a closet homophobe, and then I'm really done.

"Homo."

No reaction.

"*You* didn't write it, did you?" he asks.

I can feel my cheeks going red. "No. I was covering it up, that's all."

"And why is that?"

For a second, I'm quiet. I have no idea why, except that I didn't want Rob to see it. "It was mean," I say finally.

He picks his spotless nails, thinking.

"Whose locker is it, exactly?"

"Rob Allen."

"Ah. Mr. Allen."

I look straight at him, but he doesn't give me an inch about what he's thinking. He is definitely not surprised. Either he thinks Rob is gay and won't help, or he just knows that Rob gets picked on. Why doesn't he do something about it? Isn't that his job? I decide to remind him.

"I don't know whether or not it's true, but Rob doesn't

need it written on the front of his locker. It's none of any-body's business, right? Besides, this school is supposed to be a Bully-Free Zone, isn't it?" The sour thought is out of my mouth before I can stop it. "We have posters and everything."

He stares for a few seconds without saying any-thing. Maybe he doesn't like my "tone." He glances back at the screen and scrolls through some details.

"You're new this year, Miss Sanchez, and yet I notice you're already starting to collect tardies and detentions. You cut study hall two days ago. Not a very good start. Any reason you're having trouble getting to class?"

"No."

"And you like school so far? Things going well?"

I pick at my chipped nail polish, thinking.

"I liked my old school better," I say carefully. If I tell him about Yaqui, everything will just get worse. Being a narc means you're too weak to take care of yourself. You need a grown-up to be your shield. Where will that leave me? I'll be even more of a social outcast than I am now— open season for anyone to get after me.

Just then, there's a knock on the open door behind me. For a split second, I'm relieved for the interrup-tion. But then I see it's Coach Malone. I try my best to make myself small, wiping my eyes when Mr. Flatwell looks away.

"Staff meeting at four today," Coach Malone says with all the enthusiasm of announcing a colonoscopy.

"Oh, and here's the list of wrestlers," he adds, walking over to Mr. Flatwell's desk. "Let me know which of my darlings isn't eligible." Just as he hands over his clipboard, he takes me in. "Ah. The locker artist."

Mr. Flatwell cocks his head at me, like a cat staring at a canary.

"Can I go?" I ask desperately.

"Not yet."

I keep staring into my hands while they finish their business. After Coach Malone leaves, Mr. Flatwell leans back, waiting.

"Anything else you want to tell me, Miss Sanchez? Why you liked your old school better? If you're having problems, we can try to help."

I sit in silence, refusing to let him break me. I can't trust him. Yaqui's suspension means nothing but a little vacation. What happens when she comes back from home or prison, or wherever she is? I'm no dope.

"Miss Sanchez?"

"No," I say. "I'm just still adjusting, I think."

Mr. Flatwell sighs.

"Defacing school property is a big deal," he says. "You should have reported the graffiti to a teacher and not taken it upon yourself to remove it." His voice gets lower, and he leans toward me. "We can't help unless we know what's going on."

Help? *Help?*

The ridiculousness of it all grabs me tight. My head goes light and prickly, my hands start to shake, and a little giggle ripples up my throat. Before I can stop them, tears leak down my cheeks. I can't stop giggling, no matter how hard I try.

"Is something funny?"

"No." I take a deep breath and bite my lip hard to keep from grinning. "Can I please go back to class *now*? I have work I need to make up."

Mr. Flatwell's eyes narrow. I can see he doesn't like being left out of a joke.

"Yes, but you'll need this." He hands me an official-looking disciplinary form.

"What's this?"

"You have a Saturday detention, eight fifty-five, sharp. That's the consequence for defacing property. Have your parents sign."

Suddenly I'm sober. I can practically hear Ma's shouts.

"Are you kidding me?"

"I'm not known for my jokes, Miss Sanchez."

"But . . . Saturday is my birthday," I blurt out.

"Oh." He turns to the computer screen to check my date of birth. "You're right. Happy birthday." With that, he opens a file folder and starts reading the next referral in the stack.

Now I'm desperate. "But, Mr. Flatwell, I work on the weekends — " I begin.

He doesn't look up.

"Not this one, I'm afraid. Good-bye."

CHAPTER 15

Mr. Flatwell's papers are burning a hole in my pocket as Ma and I get off the bus at the old building on Friday afternoon at six. I haven't asked Ma to sign them, but maybe I can talk Lila into it, if I can get her alone. That might be tough. When Lila throws a party, it's always mobbed.

When we get to the lobby, we find a handmade poster taped near the mailboxes. A picture of a werewolf is staring back at us.

COME TO A MASQUERADE PARTY!
RUM, MUSIC, AND BEAUTY MASKS
TONIGHT, APARTMENT 3E
AVON BY LILA FLORES

Ma sighs.

"I hate parties," she says.

The lobby door opens just as she says it, and Mrs. Halper steps out. She's holding her mailbox keys. She has Joey's same blond hair, but none of his cockiness or spark. She's a thin lady and quiet. She glances at the flyer and nods quickly at Ma.

"Hello." Ma's eyes flit to Mrs. Halper's arms, the same way mine do. Five little bruises, like black pearls, ring her wrist. "*Vamos,* Piddy," Ma says.

I hurry up the stairs, trying not to stare at Joey's apartment as we go past.

Lila's hair is still in hot rollers when she throws opens the door. She's in a clingy black dress and slippers.

"*Ay,* thank God you're here. I'm running so late!" The furniture has all been pushed to the wall, and spice-scented candles are burning everywhere. She gives Ma a look and pouts. "You guys promised me you'd wear costumes."

"I'm dressed up as an overworked shipping clerk at Attronica," Ma says drolly. She points at the Salón Corazón T-shirt that I pulled over my turtleneck. It features a picture of Gloria and Fabio rubbing noses. "And she's dressed up as a beauty shop gofer."

Lila shakes her head and turns to me. "Here. Put these on the table." She hands me a bottle of Bacardi rum and a bag of candy corn.

"You're going to get them drunk first?" Ma hangs up her coat and surveys the arrangement of bottles. "What a business strategy!"

"Don't start," Lila says, pulling on one of her rollers. "The food trays are in the kitchen." She kisses Ma on the cheek and disappears into the bathroom.

Ma puts on an apron in the kitchen and clicks her tongue when she sees the puny tray of cheese and salami.

"Give me the bags," she says.

I hand over what we picked up at the bakery on Junction Boulevard. It's two dozen ham croquettes, meat puff pastries, and a box of guava *pasteles*. Good thing she insisted we stop there before coming over. Sometimes I really think Ma has ESP.

"You have to feed people if you want them to buy," she mutters, arranging the treats on a plate. She purses her lips, considering if it's enough. "Let's cut them smaller. Where's the good knife?"

I know it's in the third drawer, but here's my chance.

"I'll ask."

Lila is leaning into the bathroom mirror, finishing her makeup.

"If you love me, sign this," I say as I close the door behind me.

She has only one eyebrow drawn in, which makes her look lopsided as she reads the detention slip.

"Nice try, *mijita*. You give that paper to Clara. She's the mommy, not me."

"Please, Lila. I got the detention for erasing the word

homo from a kid's locker." I make a cross over my heart and kiss my fingertips to prove I'm serious.

Ma's voice sails through the apartment. She's banging open drawers.

"*Caramba*, don't you have a single sharp knife, Lila?"

"Third drawer!" Lila shouts. "What's she cutting?"

"Please, please, *please* sign." I give her my most pitiful look. "Ma will flip if I show her this. Plus, she'll be grumpy for the whole party. You know what *that's* like."

She looks at me long and hard.

"I don't like all these secrets, Piddy."

"I beg you."

"You sure you were sticking up for somebody?"

"Yes."

"Because if I find out you're lying, Piddy Sanchez, Clara isn't going to be your biggest problem. I'll mash you up into a *mofongo* myself, you hear me?"

"I swear."

The doorbell rings.

"*¡Ay, caray!*" She signs my form with her eyebrow pencil and shoos me out. "Keep them busy."

By eight, the apartment is crammed with perfumed ladies, all sampling the world of Avon. I recognize a few from the block, but mostly it's a lot of Lila's customers from Salón Corazón. A few made a big fuss over Ma when they came in, since they only see each other a few times a year, when

108

Lila ropes them in for a makeup party. *Clara, I haven't seen you in forever! Oh, my God, time is so good to you. What's your secret?* Blah-blah. The worst, though, was Beba. When she saw Ma, her eyes filled up and she threw her arms around her waist.

"Clara, *mi vida!*"

Ma looked like she was being forced to kiss a smelly relative. "Hello, Beba" was all she said. She was stiff, like she wanted to be anywhere else but here.

El Gran Combo is blaring from the CD player, and it's boiling in here. Lila has the windows propped open with her old phone books, but I'm still sweating in my turtleneck. I'm stuck here at the table with a calculator, waiting to total up the orders that aren't exactly stacking up. So far, Lila has sold three lipsticks and a gold-plated chain. Meanwhile, the meat pies are flying off the trays. Lila's not worried, though. It's still early, and she has plenty of rum and time to wear them down. I grab a fistful of candy corn from a bowl and watch her work the first victim like a pro. It's a moon-faced lady I've never met. Lila's teaching her how to use blush.

"*El secreto* is to use the darker shade down here. Then you put the lighter tone up here on your *mejillas*. See?" Lila holds up a hand mirror. "Look at that those new cheekbones! You could be Penélope Cruz's sister!"

Moon Face doesn't stand a chance.

I turn away and watch the dancers for a while, but,

really, I'm thinking of Joey. No matter how many times I look out the window, I don't see him outside on the block. He must have seen Lila's poster by the mailbox; he knows I'm up here, and yet he's nowhere. What does that mean? Maybe when the trash gets full, I'll take it down and check the basement, just in case he's been waiting for me with the cats.

Meanwhile, Beba is tearing it up on the dance area, and let me tell you, her shimmy could probably get her arrested in public. She's wearing a goofy headband with little pumpkins attached by springs. Her face is cemented over with a cucumber mask, and it makes her look like an alien as she merengues in the cramped space. Part of me wishes I could get up and let loose, the way she does. But for now, I stay put and let Beba practice the fancy moves. Unfortunately, she's had a few too many visits to the Bacardi table to make twirling in her stocking feet a good idea.

Suddenly she perks up and puts a finger to her ear. A new song has caught her attention. It's a strong accordion I recognize from Lila's collection.

"¡Oye! It's Paquita la del Barrio!" she squeals. "Paquita! Paquita! Paquita!"

Instantly half the room is singing along to "Rata de Dos Patas." It's a hit in Spanish, but I have to wonder how it would do in English. *Filthy rat on two feet. You demon from*

hell! You scum of the earth! How you've hurt me. Poisonous
snake, how I despise you!

On and on with sweetness more or less like that.

Lila is singing with gusto and soon everybody's belting
it out like drunken sailors, especially the chorus, so I can't
help but join in the fun.

Beba is dancing with even more fervor now. She turns
once, twice — and then topples in my direction. My soda
goes flying, ice cubes scattering along the linoleum floor.
The spill nearly drenches the few receipts. Lila looks over
and frowns as I'm gathering things out of the way.

"*¡Comadres!*" she says. "Don't wreck the place. It's all I
got!" She winks at me. "Piddy, *mi vida*, you okay?"

"Fine." But the spill is running off the tabletop and
onto my shoes.

Beba is on all fours as she tries to scoop the ice back
into the plastic cup, but she's too tipsy to really do the job.

"Don't worry," I tell her. "I'll get it."

She grabs my hand and presses it to her green cheek.
The round spaces she's left around her eyes make her look
owlish, and her lips can barely move.

"I'm so sorry, Piddy. *Perdóname*," she says.

"Don't worry, Beba. It was a mistake, an accident."

"Yes, an accident," she repeats.

"I'll clean it up," I tell her.

She looks up, still lost in the song. I start to move

away, but she clamps me in her vise and hugs me close all at once. Her breath is boozy, and I feel like I'm being smothered in her scented bosom.

"Everyone makes mistakes." She grabs my face in both her hands and looks into my eyes like a two-bit hypnotist. "Especially with love."

I feel myself turning red, and I fidget with my turtleneck, which has pulled down a bit to show Joey's handiwork. How could she possibly know about him and me in the basement? I try to pull away, but she holds on even tighter. "We all make mistakes, Piddy," she whispers. "We all make them. Look at your poor *mami.*"

Beba doesn't get the chance to go on. Lila has tiptoed around the mess to join us. She shakes her head as she surveys the puddle.

"Beba! What will your husband say? You're drunk." She hoists her up and steadies her. "Come on. I think your face is dry." She dabs Beba's forehead to check. "Time to see if this mask took away years like it's supposed to."

With that, they make a crooked beeline to the bathroom, Beba doing a little cha-cha and giggling the whole way.

Ma is at the sink, her back to the door, when I get to the kitchen. It's much quieter in here, cooler. She used to be friends with these ladies, but you would never know it. She's been hiding in here most of the night, the party pooper as usual, coming out a few times to pick up cups and fill food trays, like a maid. Now she's in yellow rubber gloves, washing dirty plastic forks in hot water. She hates waste.

I'm about to step inside when I notice something that makes me stop. To my shock, her hips are moving in a seductive swish from left to right. I watch from the doorway for a minute to make sure the heat isn't making me see things. But no: Ma is *definitely* dancing, even if it is all by herself. I've never seen her do it before, not once. She pauses as the music moves into the piano solo. She cocks her ear and lifts her hands from the water. Her soapy fingers dance along imaginary keys as she bangs out the chords.

"Wow," I say.

She catches my reflection in the window and goes perfectly still.

"*¡Qué susto!* Don't sneak up on me like that." Ma blushes and waves a soapy hand at the stack of dirty dishes. "These women eat like horses," she says over her shoulder. "Are they buying anything at least?"

"Not much."

"Naturally." She shakes her head and dumps a few more glasses into the soapy water. "Cheapskates. What do they think? That Lila is made of money? I have a good mind to throw them all out."

"Why don't you dance out there instead?" I ask. "You're pretty good."

She keeps her eyes on the dirty water, bits of pastry floating in the gray. Still, I can see a tiny smile curling her lip. She's probably been on her feet since the morning at Attronica, though; I can tell by her circus-lady ankles.

"And who has time for dancing, little girl?"

I go to the sink and unroll a long ribbon of paper towels. Just as I turn to go, Ma grabs my arm.

"What's that?" She juts her chin at my neck.

My hand flies up, but it's already too late. My collar must have moved when I helped Beba. Worse, I've sweated off all the concealer on my neck. Ma's eyes are bloodshot as she frowns and leans in for a good look. Her face is pale the way she always looks when she's tired. But now she's furious.

"It's nothing," I say. "I have to pick up a spill, Ma. Let me go."

"I'm not stupid. That's a *chupón*. Who did that to you?"

Standing there with the wad of paper towels, I hesitate. Her grip on my arm goes tight, and water soaks through my shirt.

"You're hurting me, Ma. Let go."

But her fingers only dig in harder. "So that's where you were the other night? Rolling around with some boy like a tramp."

I yank my arm free. Now I'm the one who's mad.

"I'm not a tramp. And you don't know anything, Ma."

I'm about to add *Look who's talking about being loose* when I remember my promise to Lila. I bite my tongue and storm to the doorway, where I glare at her. "Sorry I'm not your little angel anymore."

The clock says midnight by the time the party finally winds down. It might have gone all night except somebody started banging the ceiling with a broom to complain, and Lila doesn't like trouble. In the end, Lila made three hundred bucks. She tucked a fifty in Ma's pocketbook when they hugged good-bye.

"Be patient," I hear Lila whisper to Ma. "Don't you remember what it was like to be young?"

I stare at the building as we take our seats on the bus. Ma isn't speaking to me; that much is clear. She waves back at Lila, who's watching us from her window to make sure we're okay. Lila blows a kiss in our direction and disappears behind the blinds. The world is cottony quiet to my ears as I cup my hands to the window and look outside one last time.

Ma gives me a cold look.

"Who are you looking for?" she asks.

I turn back in my seat and pretend I don't hear her.

In all that darkness, I didn't see Joey anywhere.

CHAPTER 16

I'm at the school doors promptly at 8:55 the next morning, though my eyes are barely open and I haven't even brushed my teeth. I almost didn't make it. Ma was so tired that she actually overslept. Of all days! I had to throw on the same clothes from last night and sprint to school the back way while she waited for the bus to work.

Mr. Flatwell is already waiting at our appointed meeting spot in front of the school, of course. He insists on herding his detention victims as a group, probably a warden technique he picked up in college. He's wearing a felt cap and a dark peacoat. Steam is rising from his take-out Greek coffee.

"Good morning, Miss Sanchez," he says, taking a deep sip.

I'm winded, but I can't even lean against the doors to catch my breath. They've already been pegged with eggs and shaving cream from Halloween. A starburst pattern of yolks decorates the sidewalk, too.

There are five of us, and from the corner of my eye, I can see they're nobody I want to know. There's a truck-size kid in low pants. His pockets are at the back of his knees, and his face is so blank, it's scary. There's a bleach-blond girl with sickly legs and scabby nostrils, shivering in a leather jacket, and a short kid with leopard-print ear gauges whose name, I somehow remember, is Pipo.

After a minute or two, Mr. Flatwell glances at his watch and leads us inside, past the volunteer at the "Shoot Me First" Welcome Desk, who smiles as we file pass. The front office is locked tight and dark, but the Community Programs office is open as usual. An English-as-a-second-language class is meeting at the far end of the hall. Two little Asian kids are chasing each other outside the door, probably waiting for their mothers. The teacher's nasal voice fills the empty hallway.

"Repeat! 'May I have the check, please?'"

The class mumbles it back, but it doesn't even sound close.

Mr. Flatwell unlocks our classroom, which still smells of dust and sweat. I start for the back row, but he stops me as the fluorescent lights flicker on.

"Not today, Miss Sanchez. We sit up front like a cozy family."

I glance at my companions and slide into the second seat without a word. An empty seat is beside me.

Right away, he unlocks the desk drawer and starts to

relieve us of "contraband." Phones, music, gum — all the no-no's. Talking is especially not allowed — as if any of us would seriously have something to say to one another.

"You'll have one bathroom break at ten thirty, and —"

The sound of boots clicking down the hall makes him turn. Someone arrives at the door.

"And here I was thinking you'd forgotten," Mr. Flatwell says.

When I turn to see who it is, my blood turns to ice. Yaqui Delgado is standing in the doorway. I slump lower in my seat and stare at the board, my mind racing. Didn't Darlene say she was suspended? Shouldn't she be rotting in prison right now?

"The bus was late," she says.

"The earlier one wasn't," Mr. Flatwell replies.

She starts to come in, and every hair on my arms seems to bristle. The empty seat beside me suddenly feels like a monster magnet. I can't breathe.

Mr. Flatwell raises his hand.

"You were ordered to report at eight fifty-five, Miss Delgado. It's six past nine. You'll have to serve two more Saturdays now. See me Monday."

Instantly, I want to hug him.

Yaqui, however, isn't too pleased. She's so close, I can practically smell her rage.

"That's bull. I'm only five minutes late," she says.

"Eleven," Mr. Flatwell replies. "Do your addition."

He opens a folder on his desk and starts flipping through pages. "See you next week."

"I ain't coming here next week," Yaqui says.

Mr. Flatwell looks up genially. "Well, that's *one* choice you could make. But, then, there are consequences to everything, right?"

Her cheeks are red as she turns on her worn heels to go. I sink low, but it's too late. She spots me sitting there in my dirty Salón Corazón T-shirt. Even with my eyes glued to the board, I can feel her hate as she looks me up and down. Mr. Flatwell notices something fishy, too. He looks from Yaqui to me, a bloodhound onto a scent.

"Good-bye, Miss Delgado." He moves his body between us. And with that, he shuts the door.

Somebody tried to steal Lila's purse a couple of years ago. She was walking by herself under the train trestle on 158th Street when two guys pulled up in their car and jumped her from behind. Too bad for them. She started swinging like Oscar De La Hoya and caught one guy in the nose so hard, he couldn't get to his car before his buddy sped away. She busted him up pretty good.

"I was so scared," she told us later as she was filing down her broken nails. But that's the thing about Lila. You'd never know she's scared of anything.

I'm nothing like that.

For the first hour after Yaqui leaves, I'm shaking. I

119

keep looking out the window as I try to do my assignments, daydreaming about all the things I might have
said or done that first day Vanesa found me and gave
me Yaqui's message. I could have shoved her out of the
way. I could have told her to kiss my big swaying butt.
Could have puffed myself up big and ugly like one of
those harmless desert salamanders that fight off rattle-
snakes with a bluff.

But I didn't do any of that. I took it like a sap, and
now I can't help but feel like I made a mistake. There's no
going back and redoing my rep. All I can do is watch as she
closes in.

Concentrate, I tell myself as I start working through the
stack of work I've brought with me. The heat is too high in
here, though, and it makes me feel thickheaded. Pipo must
think so, too. He keeps nodding off as he works through
the assignment that Mr. Flatwell provided to the kids with
no work. It's multiple choice from some standardized test
Pipo will probably never pass. Every once in a while, Mr.
Flatwell shakes his desk to wake him.

I force myself to plow through my work, subject by
subject, trying to calm my nerves. My assignments have
piled up worse than the time my appendix nearly killed
me. Grades close this week, I remind myself. If I turn everything in, I might avoid an ugly exorcism at Ma's hands.
Then again, who knows if I'm going to make it to the end
of this week?

I figure out my geometry as best I can in all this heat and answer four pages of questions about plant and animal cells for biology. English is last on my list. I pull out the extra-credit sheet and scan the assignments. Ms. Shepherd is the only one of my teachers with a heart big enough to offer save-your-neck extra credit. Naturally, she's dreamed up something in the Halloween mood — not surprising, considering the fake cobwebs all over her classroom for the past week. We can read *Frankenstein* or *Dracula* and take a quiz, but it will be due Monday, and I'll never finish that much reading — even if I can find the book in the library. Maybe the essay is a better idea. I wipe the sweat from my eyes and read her prompt:

> *Monsters have long been part of literature. Whether snake-headed women, vampires, or aliens from outer space, monsters have always represented the dark side of human nature. If you could invent a modern-day monster, what would it look like? Describe it. What would it represent?*

I shiver, even though my shirt is plastered to my back. The steam is hissing through the pipes as I let my mind wander, filling it up with Yaqui's hateful face. Soon my pen is scratching along the paper, the sound like mice digging in the dark.

"Miss Sanchez?"

Mr. Flatwell is standing over my desk. I look up and rub my eyes. It's 11:59. My fingers are cramped around the pencil, and my papers are rumpled and damp from where my head has been lying on them.

"You're free," he says.

When I look around, I notice that the others have already left. On my desk are six pages of my messy hand-writing that I shuffle quickly into a stack.

"English paper?"

I shake my head and shove the papers away fast. Has he been reading my stuff?

"Just an essay."

He puts on his coat and cap, not a bead of sweat on him as I collect my things. His desk is as spotless as when we arrived.

He clicks off the lights and walks to the door to wait for me. "What's the topic?"

I sling on my backpack, suddenly embarrassed.

"Nothing. It's just . . . nothing."

Dread is building in my stomach as he walks down the hall with me. What if Yaqui is waiting for me outside? The last of the ESL students are leaving and I slow my pace so they can go first. Finally, it's just Mr. Flatwell holding the door for me.

"Something the matter, Miss Sanchez?"

Sunshine is streaming through the open doorway. I

ought to be happy to be through with detention, but the thought of what could be out there cements my feet. I have to force myself to edge past him to get out.

I don't bother to put on my coat. Instead, I start jogging for the corner.

"Miss Sanchez," he calls.

I turn around, but my feet don't stop moving. My head is still thick from the heat, and I'm scared to walk home. The cold bites into me, deep like a vampire. My courage is draining like blood.

"I don't expect to see you here again," he calls.

I break into a panicked run for home.

CHAPTER 17

"You look beautiful," Lila tells me. It's my birthday, and we're out for dinner with Raúl, so she's fixed my hair, loose around the shoulders. She also lent me a pair of heels to go with the African-print dress I bought with Mitzi.

Ma scowls. She's still cranky about my hickey, and now this dress just adds to her ever-lowering opinion of me.

"Can't you smile, at least?" Ma says to me. "What's the matter? A bad day at Corazón?"

Smile? It took me all day to calm down after seeing Yaqui this morning.

Lila hands Ma a menu fast. "What looks good?" she says.

Ma is dressed up, too, which almost never happens unless someone has died. She's wearing her black dress with fake pearls. She's even wearing pointy-toed pumps. She looks so different that I almost forget it's really her — except for when she talks, of course. I think she feels the same about me. I keep catching her looking at the neckline on my dress — and the fading hickey.

That's not the only thing that's different. This is also the first time Lila has brought a date along on an outing with us. I don't know what to think. She said it was actually Raúl's idea to celebrate my birthday here. When she told him I love roast pork as much as he does, he said, "Oh, I've got the *lechón* place for her."

At first Ma said no.

"Why not?" Lila argued. "Piddy's older now. A sweet sixteen is a special night for *americanas* like Piddy. We're not doing a party. It's not like we can take her to the zoo anymore, Clara."

To be honest, I sort of miss the zoo. But I know I'm too old for it. So, instead, we're at El Rincón Criollo, in Jackson Heights. I'm not much in the mood for celebrating anything tonight, not even my sweet sixteen. Ma was more excited about last year — my fifteenth, even though I didn't do a *quinceañera*, the way some people do. That would have meant rhinestone tiaras and poufy dresses like you're a doll in a box. *No, gracias* very much. Ma didn't have the money, and I didn't have the *ganas*. Living through Mitzi's was bad enough. Her mother planned a big party at Leonard's of Great Neck Banquet Hall last year, but Mitzi is so shy that her mother had to beg people to be in her court. It was horrible.

"Kill me now," Mitzi said when I zipped her into her satin dress. She was miserable the whole night, surrounded by kids she barely knew.

I wish Mitzi were here tonight, but she's not. Her badminton team went to finals someplace out in Riverhead. She was all excited when she told me yesterday. I could hear her new friends in the background.

"We'll celebrate next weekend," she promised in a rush. We didn't even talk long enough for me to tell her the homo-locker detention saga.

It made me mad. She claims she never got my text about Yaqui ripping me off, but I don't know. Would Mitzi lie? I have so many things to tell her, but it's getting harder. She doesn't know about me and Joey and the hickey, which she will never, *ever*, believe. She always thought he was cute, but so are grizzly bear cubs, and no one is dumb enough to get into bed with one, she'd say. But lately, every time I call, she's been busy, and I wonder if maybe she doesn't really want to know about me and my problems anymore.

I try to concentrate on the positive, like the fact that we're eating somewhere fancy for once. From the outside, El Rincón Criollo looks like a dive with blackened windows. But inside, it's a different story. The hostess wears a dress and high heels, colored lights glow in the silk palms, and good music pipes through the speakers. The whole dining room smells like garlic, cumin, and melt-in-your-mouth pork chunks. I'm in heaven.

"This place has class, right?" Lila whispers to me. She waves at Raúl, who is chatting at the bar. He knows the owner, and his good friend José moonlights as the bartender. A few young guys are looking our way, probably at Lila, although one of them actually smiles at me. I turn around to make sure he isn't looking at somebody else.

It takes forever for Ma to look over the menu, even though I'm sure she can hear my stomach growling. "Let's split something," she says.

"But I'm hungry."

"These places serve too much food. You'll never eat it all. It'll be a waste."

Lila purses her lips. "*Ay, Clarita.* It's her *cumpleaños.* Let the kid eat. Raúl will pay."

Ma looks alarmed. "*De eso nada.* Absolutely *not.* I'll pay for us, or we're not eating."

I sigh.

"Fine," I mutter. "I'll split it."

"Here you go, ladies." Raúl puts down two *mojitos* and winks at Lila as he slips in beside her. Tonight I can see what all the fuss was about at Salón Corazón. Raúl is tall, and he's got muscles everywhere, even in his jaw. His short hair is spiked, and he has light-brown eyes, just like his skin. He smells like spicy aftershave, too, which is nice.

Ma complains that he's too fussy about himself—never a good sign in a man, she says. Fussy or not, though, he's cute, and, besides, you always feel safe with a guy packing a Glock.

"Oh, I love this song." Lila closes her eyes and sways to a rumba as she tilts back her glass. It's got a great piano *tumbao*. "You used to know how to play this, didn't you, Clara?"

"I don't remember," Ma sniffs.

"Let's dance, then," Raúl tells Lila. "Come on."

Lila is about to get up when she looks across the table and gives me a sly smile.

"I have a better idea. Dance with Piddy; she's amazing! I've been teaching her everything I know." She leans forward and whispers. "Give those fools at the bar something to wonder about."

I almost spit up my soda, but Raúl doesn't seem to notice. I know he'd rather have Lila in his arms, but he smiles with those big teeth, which look nice now, and holds out his hand. "My pleasure."

He's not so great on the dance floor, as it turns out. At first, I feel like a broom in his arms, with Ma watching. But finally I let the music in, and I start to relax in a way that has been hard lately. My hips start to move like they're meant to. Lila is all smiles at the table as I turn, turn, turn into my salsa without missing a single step, just like she showed me. From the corner of my eye, I can see that the guys at the bar have stopped talking. They're watching me. Even Ma looks like she's easing up, although I can't guess what she's thinking. Yaqui Delgado melts away from me, if only for a few minutes.

"That's the way!" Lila hoots, raising her glass.

Finally, when the number is done, Raúl leads me back to my seat and holds out my chair like a gentleman. My skin is shiny, and I'm sweating beneath my dress, like I've outrun some beast.

"You're right, Lila. She's a great dancer." Then he turns to Ma. "Your daughter is going to break a lot of hearts, Clara." He tilts his head toward the bar. "Maybe even some tonight."

Ma nods and studies the menu again. "Don't remind me."

The rest of the night, Lila and Raúl tell stories to make us laugh as we gorge. He says he grew up with four brothers in Washington Heights. His brothers were always in one scrape or another, which is how he first got to know cops in his neighborhood. His oldest brother, Luis, got into drugs, though, and couldn't get out. He's dead now. "That's why I'm a cop today," he says.

Ma keeps stirring her drink, listening. I'm thinking the city must be so exciting — better than Queens, anyway. We hardly ever go into Manhattan because Ma hates the subway and all its germs. I wonder, too, what it's like to live in a house with boys wrestling and making noise, what it's like to have a father or brother around all the time, even if they're trouble. Safe, I decide. It must feel safe.

Then Raúl mentions something that perks me up.

"It's a lot harder today, though. The Bland is a rough beat."

"That's your beat?" I ask. That's Yaqui's neighborhood. "You're there every day?"

Raúl nods.

"I could park the squad car on any corner and stay busy dusk to dawn, unfortunately." He shakes his head. "Last week, we found a kid shot through the head in the lobby of his building."

Ma crosses herself.

Just then José sends over refills, and our waitress appears with four individual flans. Mine has a candle sparkling from the center. The whole place sings to me an off-key "Las Mañanitas" and then "Happy Birthday" after that. Even Ma smiles and applauds when it's over.

The ride home late that night is quiet. Ma and I are in the back. Lila is sitting close to Raúl. The radio is playing a nice bolero, the kind you'd dance to slowly with someone you love. And maybe that's just what they'll do later up in her apartment. The night air is cold, but those two look toasty warm. I want to hold on to this ride forever.

130

"You ever been married, Raúl?" Ma's question seems to come out of nowhere to shatter the quiet.

I can see his handsome eyes in the rearview mirror. Ma, however, is still staring outside, like she's a million miles away.

"What?"

"Clara—" Lila starts to say.

"Married. *Ca-sa-do.* Have you ever been married?"

Raúl's smile doesn't fade, even as his eyes flit to Lila's.

"Yes. In fact, I was married—a long time ago."

"Where's your wife now?"

"Ma," I mumble. How is this her business?

"*Ex*-wife," he says. "She lived in Bayside last time I knew. Why?"

Lila is blushing, and it feels like the air is going to explode into a ball of fire.

"No reason," Lila says firmly as she cranes her neck to look at Ma severely. "Clara is my best friend. She's just being nosy."

Ma finally turns from the window to meet Lila's gaze, but she doesn't say anything else. She looks so sad; the little lines around her mouth are showing.

The rest of the ride home is quiet except for the music on the radio, the magic ruined by a poison no one names.

"Thanks for the *lechón*," I tell Raúl when he drops us off at the curb a little while later. I lean in the window to say good-bye. "It was delicious."

"No problem. Thanks for the dance," Raúl says.

Lila looks past me at Ma, who has already climbed out. Then she pulls me toward her and gives me a big kiss.

"Te quiero mucho," she says.

I hurry for the door, but Lila calls to me just before I step inside behind Ma. "Happy sixteenth, Piddy."

I turn and wave as their headlights disappear down the road, their private bolero fading on the air.

CHAPTER 18

There's only one bathroom at DJ that you can use without risking somebody messing with you, at least according to Darlene. It's the one by the main office. And wouldn't you know my luck—the custodian has blocked it off with his buckets. Darlene starts to step inside, but he stops us with his mop that reeks of disinfectant.

"Toilet overflowed," he says, pointing at the puddle oozing out the door. "Use the locker rooms."

Darlene cuts him with her eyes. "Right." Then she turns to me. "We'll go to the nurse's office next hour. Say you're having your period, and they'll let you in."

All things considered, it has been pretty calm this week. Yaqui is still serving her suspension, although I found out it's an *in-school* suspension, which isn't nearly as comforting. Still, she's been penned up on the second floor, far from anywhere I need to be. I handed in my work on Monday, and I've been on time to every class. I try my best not to think about next week, when Yaqui will be free again. That really makes me want to pee.

"Hi, Piddy," Rob says when we walk into English. He's been staring at me even more than usual, so I have to wonder if he knows I was the one who scribbled on his locker. Darlene hustles me past him fast.

"God, he's so revolting," she whispers.

"Hi, Rob," I say anyway.

"Seats, everyone." Ms. Shepherd is handing back work. If I did a decent job on the extra-credit essay, I might manage to get a low B on my report card, despite the string of zeroes. Ma won't like it, but it will be better than the D that I was really supposed to get, which would set her hair on fire. Darlene is beaming over her A paper and filing it away in her color-coded binder. I wait for Ms. Shepherd to finish giving out papers, but when she reaches the end of the stack, my desk is still empty. I'm positive I handed it in.

"Where's mine?" I ask.

She turns around and studies me for a second. Maybe it wasn't good? When I think back on it, I think I was delirious as I wrote that essay in Mr. Flatwell's detention. In fact, the thought of it suddenly makes me cringe. The monster I described was a Yaqui. It's disguised as a girl — a school-yard girl with a tight bun and steely eyes who eats people's hearts for no good reason. I even gave her pointy teeth, a fat ass, and bad skin.

But Ms. Shepherd slowly breaks into a wide smile.

"Well, there's good news — and now is a good time to share it. I've submitted the strongest writing this marking period to the school magazine. Yours was included."

"Since when do we have a school magazine?" Darlene says.

"Since right now," Ms. Shepherd continues. "This class will serve as the first editorial committee. In fact, I already have a managing editor in mind."

Darlene holds up her hand to stop her. "I'm sorry, Ms. Shepherd. I'm too busy to manage a school magazine this term."

Ms. Shepherd smiles. "Actually, I asked Rob if he would serve as managing editor this semester."

Darlene starts gaping like a bass out of water. When I look at Rob, I can see his ears have turned bright pink. I look from him to Ms. Shepherd in a panic.

"Where's my essay?" I say again.

"The essays we've chosen are posted on the English department bulletin board as a teaser for our first issue," she says, beaming. She puts her hand on mine. "Great piece on monsters."

This can't be happening. If anyone sees that essay and has half a brain, they might recognize the real monster I'm talking about. Then I'm dead for sure.

"I need it back," I tell her.

"It will only be up for a week or so. I'll give it back after that. I promise."

I shake my head. "I don't want my work up there."

"Why not?" she asks gently. "You're an excellent writer. You can be proud —"

"Because it's private!" My voice is shrill, and it probably sounds like I'm being a brat. "Because I don't want my work on that board. You should have asked me!"

"Calm down, Piddy," Ms. Shepherd says. "We can discuss this after class."

"No. I need my essay back right now. Where is the bulletin board?"

Everyone is watching us. Ms. Shepherd puts her hands on her hips and stands her ground. She's nice, but even she has her limits.

"Well, you're not going to get it back *right* now. I'll be happy to return it — *after* class. We'll discuss it then."

I seethe all hour long. Shouldn't she have asked my permission? But really, I have only myself to blame. What was I thinking? My only hope is that no one has seen it — especially not Yaqui or any of her friends.

Still.

When the bell rings, Ms. Shepherd calls me to her desk, but I bolt out the door instead. I don't know what bulletin board she could mean or where it is, but I have to find it fast. I push through the crowds, checking the whole first floor for the display, but find nothing except an old trophy case with plaques from the 1990s. Then I remember that the English department office is on the second floor, not too far from the in-school suspension room. I take the steps two at a time and get there gasping for breath. Ms. Shepherd has advertised for the new magazine in big glittery letters that no one can miss. The board has already been trashed with doodles and tags, the corrugated border hanging off in a long ribbon. All the essays are stapled here. I scan them as fast as I can, but I don't find mine. I look again more slowly, even though the warning bell has sounded. Then my heart sinks. Near the center of the board is a white space. Two staples are still attached to the ripped corners of loose-leaf paper, but the rest of the sheet has been ripped away.

My essay has been taken.

"Clear the halls," someone barks.

I watch everyone's eyes at lunch, especially Yaqui's table. I don't say a word to anyone.

"What is your problem?" Darlene asks. I haven't told her what my essay said. "You have your period or something?"

I throw away my food uneaten and wait in silence for the stairwell doors to open. That's when the kids from in-school suspension will get walked through the lunch line with their teacher on duty. Maybe I'll be able to see from Yaqui's face if she knows what I've written.

Rob slides in next to me.

Darlene glares. "Oh, good. It's Rob."

"Shut up," I tell her.

Darlene looks surprised, but she shrugs and takes a swig of her water.

Just then the door swings open, and the parade of detention kids begins. They're trailing Coach Malone, who looks about as enthused for this duty as he does for faculty meetings. There are only four kids with him today, three guys and Yaqui. I swear all that's missing are the ankle shackles. I pretend to reach for my binder, but my eyes are glued to Yaqui as she struts forward.

"Ya-qui," someone shouts from her table. It's Alfredo. A catcall goes up.

She grins, even when Coach Malone gives her a warning look. As they go through the line, I watch Yaqui and the others grab their sporks and napkins.

When Yaqui finally steps out into the cafateria, she looks around the cafeteria. Her eyes go steely when she catches me staring, but I can't tell if she knows something or if that's her normal hateful look. The sight of her sears itself into my imagination. Even after she and the others are gone, my eyes still see her.

A few minutes later, the bell finally rings. Rob starts to follow me.

"Piddy," he calls, trying to catch up as I reach the stairs. I grit my teeth and pretend I don't hear him. I just can't bring myself to be nice to anyone right now. Only two more hours and I can get out of here. I just want school to be over. I want to be home.

But Rob is determined. I'm halfway up the steps when he catches my elbow.

"Piddy. I want to tell you something."

I whip around, suddenly irritated. His pinched face is more than I can stand. He looks weak and loathsome. He's everything I don't want to be.

"Look, Rob, nothing personal. I just really want to be left alone."

He turns bright red and swallows hard. "But —"

"Please go away." I start to go, but he reaches for my hand.

"Stop it!" I snatch back my hand and even give him a little shove. "Can't you take a hint!" I don't know which one of us is more surprised. Then his face darkens and he drops something at my feet before hurrying off.

When I look down, my knees go a little weak, and I'm filled with shame as I pick it up. It's my essay, folded neatly into a little square. The top corners are torn, but other-wise it's all here. He must have known and taken it down.

Now who's the jerk?

Rob is already on the next landing as the warning bell sounds.

"Hey!" I shout, running after him. "Come back!" But it's too late. Rob has activated his personal force field against attack, and I can't get through.

I tear the essay to bits and head off, late once again.

CHAPTER 19

"It never pays to owe anybody anything," Ma always says. Now I see she's right.

I check the address on the building doors against the slip of paper Darlene gave me. I'd hoped she might have a heart and forget the deal we made when she filched Yaqui's schedule for me. I should have known better. She caught up with me yesterday, after Ms. O'Donnell announced our unit test on vectors.

"We had a deal," she said when I tried to get out of it. "My house — tomorrow. Here's the address."

Her building still has its name in gold letters over the entrance: THE GLEN ORA. It has a slate walkway, a mirrored lobby, and a porter who actually remembers to clip the shrubs and sweep away cigarette butts. It must have been a luxury building once. They still have doctors' offices on the first floor and everything. Still, it hasn't been totally spared. Faded graffiti shows through the painted walls under the intercom.

As soon as I step off the elevator on the sixth floor, I find Darlene waiting for me at her apartment door. She looks at her watch to remind me that I'm ten minutes late.

"That's Cleopatra," she says, leading me inside. "She's sixteen." An old tabby growls at me from the sofa. You can see every bone on its spine. Darlene heads down the hall. "This way."

Her bedroom is small but nice. All the furniture matches, and the carpet still smells new. Naturally, she has a collection of trophies and laminated award certificates going back to grade school. Her desk is by a large window overlooking the street. From way up here, the parked cars and trees look organized, planned. The air is quiet.

Darlene flops down on her bed, where her physics textbook is open.

"I despise Ms. O'Donnell," she says. "She's the worst teacher I've ever had." Darlene holds up the most recent quiz; a red 72 is circled. She picks up the book and reads the first question aloud.

"A roller coaster named the Steel Dragon starts with an initial velocity of three meters per second at the top of a large rise and attains a velocity of forty-two point nine meters per second when it reaches the bottom. If the roller coaster were to start at the bottom of the rise, what would its velocity be at the top? Friction is negligible." She looks up at me in disgust. "Seriously. Who even cares?"

"Not me."

"Do you have the answers?" she asks.

I dig into my pocket for my homework and hand it over. "I worked them out last night."

Darlene raises her eyebrows and giggles as she scans my answers. "I'll change the words so they don't look exactly the same."

"Not so fast," I say, snatching them back. Nothing would make me happier than to get out of here. Still, I'm not the luckiest person, and this could go wrong in a big way. "I was supposed to help you study," I say. "Not cheat."

"I am *not* a cheater."

I take a deep breath. "Okay, tell me this. What are you going to do if O'Donnell asks you to explain how you got the answer? Cheating is an honor-code violation or something, isn't it?"

"It's a level-two offense," she says importantly, but I can tell she's reconsidering. I give her the clincher.

"If we're caught, you'll lose your student-aide job and get stuck in study hall."

For the next hour, we plow through kinetic and potential energy, velocity, and gravity. It's not easy. I have to keep reminding her that what she calls "common sense" is not compatible with scientific logic.

"Look," I tell her. "Forget what you think should

happen. The real world doesn't work that way." We work on the laws of gravity again. When we're finally through, she leans back.

"Not bad."

"What?"

"Your science skills. I assume you'll apply to McCleary."

I stand up to get my coat. "What's McCleary?"

She rolls her eyes.

"J. C. McCleary. I gave you the application, stupid. It's the science magnet school for juniors and seniors. You get college credit while you're still in high school. I hear they have good engineering programs, if you don't mind the geeks. You might be smart enough to get in." She considers me for a second. "Plus you have that Latina advantage for admission."

It would be nice to bash her skull right about now. "I don't want to be an engineer," I say.

"Let me guess. You're going to be a writer. Maybe join Ms. Shepherd's stupid magazine." Her lips curl down as she says it. I think she's still sore about not being chosen as the managing editor. She actually looks hurt, although maybe it's just Rob being chosen that's killing her. With Darlene, pride is everything.

"I'm not joining the magazine," I say.

She nods thoughtfully. "I know—who'd want to be on her stupid editorial team? My God, *Rob* at the helm."

"It's not that," I say firmly.

She grips her pillow and leans back on the bed. "Then, what are you doing after DJ?" When I don't answer, she leans in. "My parents want me to study accounting at Hofstra"—she pretends to stick her finger down her throat—"but I'm going to run my own company. My aunt owns a purse company. I work in the office every summer. She says I'm a natural leader."

"Oh." The thought of Darlene with unlimited authority is bone-chilling. "That makes sense."

"So? How about you?"

I've never told anybody except Mitzi what I want to be, and I'm not inclined to tell Darlene. You can't trust your dreams to just anybody, much less a terminal realist like her. "I want to study animals." I stand up and grab up my coat.

"You? A vet?"

My eyes slide to Cleopatra, who found her perch on the windowsill a while ago. Her arthritic paws shake as she tries to wash her ears.

"Sort of," I say.

She scoops up Cleopatra and walks me to the door. "Piedad Sanchez, veterinarian. I've heard crazier things."

"See ya, Darlene," I say as I edge past her.

"McCleary has biology, too," she calls.

I give her an icy look as the elevator door closes.

145

CHAPTER 20

I'm sweeping up hair at Salón Corazón on Saturday. Mountains and mountains of hair in every color. Gloria is running a shampoo, cut, and blow-dry special for twenty dollars during November, so the place is jammed. It seems like every Latina in Queens is trying to squeeze in an appointment before Turkey Day. Even Lila is having trouble keeping up. I wish Thanksgiving would get here already. It's not just the food. I love Ma's turkey, though I'm sure no Pilgrim ever ate it with a side of fried bananas like we do. The real treat will be four days without DJ. Maybe Mitzi will come over, if she ever calls me back.

I'm crouched over the dustpan when Gloria taps me on the shoulder and whispers in my ear.

"Friends of yours?"

I follow her gaze through the plate-glass window to the sidewalk outside. A group of girls is sitting on the hood of a parked car. It's Vanesa and the lunchroom Latinas. How do they know where I work? Then I remember what

I was wearing in detention, and I realize Yaqui is smarter than she looks. She could have figured it out from my T-shirt easily enough. But why are these girls here now? This can't be good.

"They've been waiting for a while," Gloria tells me as she fixes a fresh plate of cookies for the reception area. "You can go talk to your friends, but don't be too long. We're so busy today, *mi vida.*"

"They're not my friends." My feet are rooted to the spot as I stare.

"No? Then see if they want to come in. We can't have them looking like vagrants out there. It's bad for business." She purses her lips. "That skinny one could use a new haircut, if you ask me." The phone rings, and she turns to answer it. "*Buenos días,* Salón Corazón . . ."

My hands grip the broom handle as I head for the door. Instinctively, my eyes dart along the street. Yaqui is nowhere, but Vanesa is motioning to me to come outside. She's in a fake fur jacket, snapping gum.

Fabio starts to run circles around my feet, and I have to push him away with my broom.

"Not now," I tell him, but as soon as I open the door, he darts out, anyway. He fixes the girls with his cloudy stare and starts to sniff at their feet carefully. Right now, I wish he were a Doberman or a Rottweiler — anything scarier than the annoying little ball of fur that he is.

Once I'm outside, I stand in front of the window where

people can see. I've got my broom held tight in case I have to crack somebody on the head, Lila-style.

"What?" I say.

Vanesa gets right to business.

"Yaqui wants to fight," she says.

I try not to sound scared, even though my knees feel soft and my mouth is dry. "You're her little messenger?"

"Today," Vanesa says, ignoring my question.

"I'm not going to fight Yaqui," I say. "Not today or ever. I haven't done a thing to her."

Vanesa takes a step closer. "You think you're all that, Miss Bitch? You think you're so smart? You think you can shake your tight white ass for all the guys? Where's your respect?"

"Respect for who? Somebody who steals my stuff and throws milk cartons at me? Right. Tell her I'm not coming."

She laughs. "You scared?"

"No. I'm *working*." I motion at the obvious, and narrow my eyes to look mean. "It's busy here today."

"Be at Bowne Park at six."

Bowne Park is up near Northern Boulevard, not too far from here — or from the Bland. When I was little, Ma would push me on the swings and hold down the seesaw on one side. I think of the alleys in between the buildings over there, how it's starting to be dark around that time.

"No."

"You don't show up, she's gonna find you anyway.

And then she'll put more pain on you for real."

Until now, Fabio has been on a simmering growl. Without warning, he erupts into loud yapping that lifts his stumpy front legs off the ground with each bark. His teeth are bared, but it just makes him look more ridiculous. Vanesa rolls her eyes.

That's when the bells on the door jangle and Lila steps outside. She wipes her hands on a towel, scoops up Fabio, and puts him inside. Then she steps close to Vanesa and me. She takes in Vanesa head to toe with an expression on her face I've never seen before.

"Who's this?" she asks without a smile.

I don't know how to answer. Part of me is panicking, and part of me is relieved.

"Vanesa is just leaving." I turn my back to the girls and talk over my shoulder. "Like I said, I'm busy today."

Vanesa's eyes go from me to Lila.

"See you another time, then," she says. The other girls slide from the hood of the car and follow her across the street to the corner fruit stand. Lila holds her ground and watches.

"You coming?" I hold open the door for her. "It's cold."

But Lila doesn't answer. She keeps her eyes on the group as they disappear around the block. She doesn't even blink when Vanesa gives her the finger.

"What's going on, Piddy?" she asks.

"Come on," I say, hurrying inside. The phone is ringing like crazy. Hair is piling up everywhere.

"Piddy, sweep up station two, *por favor,*" Gloria says.

Lila is right behind me. She peers at the appointment book, but I can tell she's thinking about my mystery
visitors.

"Who's next on the list to get gorgeous?" she asks.

Of course I don't go to Bowne Park.

After work, I'm still shaken up about Vanesa's visit. I
tell Lila my feet are too tired for walking and she agrees.
She washed eighty heads today, a record. We pick up
Korean food and head home on the bus.

"So, you gonna tell me about those girls?" she asks me
on the ride.

I keep my eyes on the world going by us outside.
"They're just girls from school. They wanted me to meet
them someplace, but I don't like them. They're jerks."

"No kidding," she says. "Stay away from them."

"I'm trying."

When we get to her door, we find that an Avon shipment has arrived. It's the merchandise to fill the orders
from her party. The box is enormous, and she'll need my
help breaking it up.

I watch the clock as we work to check each item against
the forms and fill the plastic bags for each customer.
Five o'clock: lipsticks and mascara for Amada Lopez down

150

the street. Five ten: one body splash and earrings for Beba. Five twenty: skin-firming mask for Maria Estela. And on like that. The whole time, I keep wondering who is waiting for me at Bowne Park. What will they do when they realize I'm really not going to show for our appointment?

We work all the way until nine o'clock. Finally, Lila stretches her back and stares at the mess of bags and receipts all over the floor. Then she looks over at me.

"You better go home and get some sleep, *chica*. You're too young to look so tired," she says. I glance out the window. It's just a few stops up the road to our new place, but I've been worrying that Yaqui will be waiting for me.

Lila joins me.

"You know what?" she says quietly. "I need some fresh air, too. How about if I ride a few stops on the bus with you?"

Relief washes through me as she kisses my shoulder and slips some new lipstick samples in my pocket.

"If you want," I whisper. "Thanks."

The living-room light is still on when I get home. Ma is upstairs, having nodded off in front of the TV. She's braless in her housecoat, her lips hanging open. A plate of what's left of fried eggs and white rice is sitting on a box nearby.

I don't wake her up. I put her dish in the sink and cover her up. Then I slip inside the bathroom and lock the door to think. It feels like anchors are weighing down on me.

What am I going to do? It's only a matter of time before I have to face Yaqui and her cronies.

I run the water hot and strip off my clothes. Then I stare at myself long and hard in the mirror. I hate the slopes and curves; they've caused nothing but trouble. If having a body is so great, why has it made such a mess for me?

I pull back my hair to put on the shower cap and stop. It suddenly occurs to me that this is not so different from how Yaqui wears her hair. I fish through Ma's drawer for hairpins and finish fastening it in place. I don't step into the shower. Instead, I search my pants pockets and find one of Lila's lipstick samples. It's a dark burgundy that Ma would never let me wear. Slowly I draw in my lips. Then I dig under the sink for Ma's ancient makeup bag and find her tweezers. I work carefully, painfully. My eyebrows grow thinner and thinner until I'm teary and my skin is red and swollen, until there is only the barest line remaining. When I'm done, I stand back and inspect myself again. I look expressionless and strangely vicious. If Ma walked by me, she might never recognize me at all. *That's not my daughter,* she'd think.

And she'd be right.

Maybe this is the new me I need to find. A girl tough enough to face Yaqui. But if that's true, why do I still feel afraid?

152

CHAPTER 21

I don't tell Mitzi I'm coming. It will be a surprise. We were supposed to get together this weekend — a rain check for my birthday. I'll sit in her room and tell her everything. She'll know what I should do.

Ma didn't try to stop me when I told her I was going. She calls Mitzi a *good influence*. Maybe she thought that's what I needed right now, considering my recent cosmetic handiwork.

"What have you done?" she asked when she saw me this morning. She put down her cup of coffee and shook her head. "What's happening to you?"

"I don't know," I told her honestly.

The bus hums along Northern Boulevard for a long while, but eventually the wooded neighborhoods after Great Neck take over, each one blending into the next. There are fewer people on the streets out here, fewer kinds of people, too. Everything looks clean. I sit by myself in the back, staring out the window as the world outside gets more peaceful with each passing mile. I ride by Italian delis and bakeries, by cobblers and candy stores. I can't help but wonder if Mitzi remembers what it's like back in Queens. Sometimes I wonder if she's starting to forget me, too.

It takes longer than I thought to get there — almost two hours, including waiting for the bus transfer — but I find the address okay. It's a small house, a few blocks off the main avenue. It's one of those doll-size things with a pointy roof, like something out of "Hansel and Gretel."

For a second, Mrs. Ortega doesn't recognize me when she opens the door. She frowns a little, but then her eyes go wide.

"Piedad! Is that you?" She holds the door wide. Mrs. Ortega is a small woman with jet-black hair and sparkly eyes. She's a plump, old version of Mitzi. She crushes me in a hug.

"Come in, come in! Did Mitzi forget you were coming?"

I shake my head and pull down my hood. The house feels warm compared to outside. It smells of garlic and roasting meat; the Ortegas have a Sunday-afternoon dinner every week, so I knew Mitzi would be home.

"No. It's a surprise."

"¿Sí? Well, that's perfect. You'll stay to eat, then. But why don't you go find her? She's at the basketball court with Sophia and some other girls."

"Who's Sophia?"

"Mitzi's new friend," she boasts. "They're practicing for basketball. Tryouts are coming up."

My heart squeezes a little, even though Mrs. Ortega looks so happy at the prospect, I think she might burst.

"Mitzi doesn't play basketball," I point out. She's always hated to run on account of her chest and the endless jokes.

"She does now. Can you imagine it? She might be part of the team!"

She walks me out to the stoop and points up the street. "It's three blocks that way and then a left. You can't miss it — Saint Ana's. You'll see the girls on the court."

My feet feel heavy as I go.

I hear the girls playing before I actually see them. They're grunting and laughing, trash-talking a little. I hang back near the bushes to watch. Saint Ana's is a pretty church with a few school buildings attached. Beside them is a carpet of soccer fields surrounded by a track. There are five girls on the basketball courts besides Mitzi. From the looks of it, Mitzi is playing point guard — badly.

"Arms up, Ortega!" one of them shouts, slipping around Mitzi for the shot. It's all net. The other girls cheer.

"Ugh," Mitzi says. "I am never going to make it."

"Don't say that!" a bushy-haired girl says. "We have two weeks to get you ready. That's plenty of time." She's plain-faced but pretty. Her curly hair is in a ponytail, and she's wearing track pants and Under Armour, like someone in an ad for health food or yoga.

Just as they're about to set up again, I step out.

"Hi."

Mitzi looks at me blankly for a second, like she can't recognize me at all. I pull down my hood and smile.

"Piddy?" she says.

"Surprise!"

Mitzi drops the ball and comes running over.

"Hi! Oh, my God, what are you doing here?"

I shift my weight uncomfortably as the other girls turn to watch us. She's forgotten we were supposed to get together, but at least she looks happy that I'm here.

"Nothing. Just thought we were going to hang out this weekend."

Mitzi smiles brightly and gives me a hug. Then she turns to the others.

"Come meet everybody. This is Heather, Miranda, Chloe, Olive, and Sophia. Everybody, this is Piddy."

"Hi," I manage. I've never seen Mitzi talk to so many people at once. It makes her seem like a stranger to me. "Basketball, huh?" I say.

Mitzi blushes. "Yeah." She lowers her voice a little. "We're almost done here, I think. A few minutes more. We're getting ready for —"

"Tryouts. Yeah. Your mom told me."

It sounds like an accusation, even though I don't mean it that way. I glance around at the girls. They're all nice enough, but I can feel them trying to make sense of me, my clothes. Mitzi is studying my face, maybe even noticing my new brows. I'm noticing things about her, too. Her sneakers are blindingly white and new, for one thing.

I look out at the fields.

"It's like a country club out here, huh? Peaceful."

Mitzi looks embarrassed. "I guess."

Sophia, who's been listening, comes to stand closer.

"We're going to get something to eat. You can come, too, Patty," she says politely.

"Piddy," I say. My rudeness surprises even me, but I don't know the first thing about Sophia or any of these girls, and that alone makes me uncomfortable. "No, thanks."

"Piddy—" Mitzi begins, frowning a little.

"It's just that your mom invited me to dinner," I add quickly to soften things.

Mitzi turns to Sophia and offers a pained smile. "I'm sorry, guys. I have to be home for dinner. Do you mind if I cut out early?"

I can feel their stares on our backs all the way down the block. It's as though I've walked off with their prize.

The rest of the night is hard for Mitzi and me. I know it's my fault. I pick at my dinner as Mrs. Ortega chatters away about Mitzi's this-club and that-club. When she asks me how school is, all I can offer is a lame "Fine." What am I supposed to say?

Later, when we're eating ice cream in her room, I can't bring myself to tell Mitzi what's been going on. It makes me feel like a loser to tell her about Yaqui when her own life is going so great out here.

When it's time to leave, she walks me to the bus stop, her hands shoved deep into her pockets. It's almost dark out, and I can hardly see her face. Still, I know the look she's wearing. The corners of her lips are down.

"You're acting really different," she says.

"No, I'm not."

"You're hardly talking. You looked at all the stuff in my room like you're a crime detective."

"Actually, you're the one who's different. I'm still in Queens, remember, Mitzi? Same as always." It comes out harsher than I want.

Mitzi stops walking. "But you're not the same."

"The same as what? *You're* the one who moved out here and got all new snooty friends, not me. I've been calling you for, like, two weeks."

"They're *not* snooty. And what's wrong with making new friends, Piddy? You want me to sulk about a new school and be all alone?"

I give her an ugly look.

"Are you saying I'm sulking? Is that what you think?"

158

"I'm saying that if you'd give Sophia and them a chance, you'd see they're smart and nice. Which is more than I can say for you right now. What's with you, anyway? Look at you!" She points at my hair, my face. "You even *look* mean."

In all my life, I've never wanted to hurt Mitzi, but if I could clock her right now, I would. Thankfully, my bus rounds the corner. I wave my hand to flag it down, taking off at a jog.

"Nothing's wrong, Mitzi. Nothing at all." I'm practically shouting. "Everything is just perfect. Why don't you just forget me and enjoy your new life."

And with that, I'm on my way home.

CHAPTER 22

I should have noticed them waiting at the corner, but the girls are tucked far inside the doorway of the apartment building, and I don't see them until I go by. They've been smart; I'll give them that. It's Friday. All week, no one messed with me. I should have known it was too good to believe.

When I pass by, they slip out and follow me down the block like a wolf pack organizing their hunt.

I walk faster, trying to get home as soon as I can, but somewhere deep inside I already know it's too late. They're giggling behind me. Someone tosses a rock. A voice whispers, "Bitch."

Nearly jogging now, I'm close enough to my front yard that I can see the dying edges of Mrs. Boika's rosebushes. But it's no use. All at once, Yaqui rushes up from behind and grabs a fistful of my hair. She yanks my head back until my feet tangle. Vanesa holds up her phone, recording my face. *Click, click, click.* Someone yanks my jacket right off my back.

Yaqui is a rabid boxer, her fists balled. I tower over her by several inches, but not even my size helps. She's done this before. I kick and try to twist out of her grip, but nothing stops her from toppling me and pressing my face into the pavement. She kicks me hard in the ribs as her friends say, "Ooh," and cover their mouths to laugh.

"Stop! Let me go!" I yell.

I'm fighting with all my might, scraping my nails deep along her arms, but I'm in no-man's-land now. Though Daniel Jones is still in sight, I'm off school grounds and there are no crowds to help, just passersby who stop, point. Only a cop can save me now, and there's none around. Mrs. Boika looks out her kitchen curtains in shock, but she's too scared to move.

Yaqui lifts me from the ground by the hem of my shirt and yanks it straight over my head so I can't see. I kick blindly. The girls are hooting even louder as I fight to keep my arms in the sleeves. She's not going to steal the shirt off my back.

Then the fabric tears, and with a sickening rip, I go hurtling to the ground half naked. I run for my door and pound. My hands are shaking too hard to find my key.

"Let me in, Mrs. Boika! Please!" I scream.

Yaqui lunges again. I can feel the rage in each slap and bite; it's like I'm being devoured alive. Finally, she reaches for my total humiliation. She rips off one of my lacy bra straps and pulls the remaining shreds down around my waist. I'm left huddled in my doorway cupping my hands over my breasts, wearing only my jeans for all of Parsons Boulevard to see. Drivers slow down and crane their necks.

When she's done, Yaqui wraps my shirt around her shoulders like a towel. She's out of breath and glowing. Strands of her hair have come loose around her face, and she wears the bloody scratches with pride. She's victorious — almost beautiful even.

"Want this?" She gives me one final shove and drops something to the pavement. It's my broken elephant necklace, which she grinds into the pavement. "Keep away from Alfredo." Then she walks off with her friends, a slow promenade up the street.

Lila takes one look at my face and steps inside, out of breath. Her fingers are still wrinkled from the sinks at Corazón. I called the salon as soon as I got inside. "It's an emergency!" I screamed at Gloria. "Tell Lila to come now."

She grabs my hand and leads me straight to the bathroom without a word. Yanking aside the shower curtain, she points at the edge of the tub.

"Sit."

I'm shaking all over, from a pain I've never known before. Pebbles are pressed deep inside my scrapes. Lila works my cheeks and palms with a soapy washcloth trying to lodge the grit free. I start to cry all over again.

"*Sh, sh, sh, sh* . . ." It's her nervous sound, the same noise a pressure cooker makes. As she turns me, like a seamstress fitting her model, she studies the little circles of teeth on my shoulders, the welts on my ribs. She stops at the long pink scrape across my back from the bra hook. Her lips narrow to white lines. "Take off the rest of your clothes."

The last time someone saw me naked, I was six. I hold my hands over my breasts as Lila dissolves a handful of Epsom salts in the full blast of the tub faucet.

"Take a deep breath and hold it. It's gonna sting for a second, but it's the only way to get this mess clean," she says, helping me in.

I crouch in the water with my knees to my chest. It's like alcohol on a paper cut. Lila holds me still as I try to get out.

"Wait. It's going to be better in a second."

I squeeze my eyes tight until every burning scrape starts to feel numb. When I finally settle into the pain, she sits down on the edge of the tub and lights up a cigarette. At first, she doesn't say anything.

"What *puta* did this to you?" she finally asks. "The one who came to Corazón?"

"Her friend. A girl named Yaqui," I say.

"Yaqui who?"

"Delgado. She's from the Bland."

Lila takes a long drag, thinking.

"You take her boyfriend?"

"No!"

She lets the smoke out slowly through her nostrils.

"Please don't tell Ma," I whisper. "Promise me."

Lila looks down at me.

"Are you crazy? We *have* to tell Clara."

Water sloshes over the side as I lunge for Lila's hand. Getting Ma involved scares me more than Yaqui does.

"No! You can't tell her!"

Lila's pants are soaked, but she doesn't move from the puddle I've made all around her.

"And how do you think you're going to explain your face, Piddy?" She flicks her cigarette butt into the toilet. "You look like you kissed a runaway truck, in case you don't know."

I start bawling. I know she's right.

"Don't you see? Ma will go to school. She'll make a *scene*, Lila — in front of everybody. You know what happens then? I'll get dragged to the dean's office with Yaqui to shake her hand and say sorry, because nobody ever gets expelled at DJ, no matter what they do."

"Sit down. Calm yourself —"

I'm crying hard now, and my voice echoes too loudly off the tile.

"I won't sit down. Don't tell me to calm down! Yaqui will just get me worse the next time — her or one of her friends. I swear to God, if you tell Ma, you're digging my grave."

I scramble over the side of the tub and grab for a towel to cover myself.

"I've kept your secret about Ma and my father. Now you have to keep mine. If you don't, I'll hate you forever."

Lila doesn't follow as I run to my room and slam the door shut.

By the time Ma's keys jangle in the door, I'm at the kitchen table, my hands cupped around a mug of tea to keep them steady. Lila has boiled rice and opened a can of beans for Ma. I tug on the sleeves of my clean sweatshirt to make sure I'm covered and she can't see all the places I've been hurt.

At first, Ma doesn't notice a thing except the stink of cigarettes. She shakes her head when she sees Lila smoking at the kitchen table. The ashtray is overflowing.

"*Cristo,* how many times do I have to tell you? Piddy is allergic to smoke. And you're gonna get a cancer!" She waves her hands to clear the smoke and is about to pull the butt from Lila's lips when she gets her first good look at me. Her face goes pale as she reaches for her own throat.

165

"*¡Ave Maria purísima!* What happened to you?" She comes at me, hands outstretched. "*¡Dime qué te pasó!*"

She tries to touch my swollen eyelid, but I turn away in time.

"It was the stupid stairs," I say. "I slipped and hit my face on the end of the handrail. Thank God Lila came by after work. " Every breath hurts as I speak. "Nothing's broken."

Ma looks from me to Lila.

"You fell down the stairs." It's not a question. Ma is no dummy, and her wheels are whirling. I can smell her doubt. I can almost see a hundred pictures of me on Attronica TV screens, my face made a pulp. She walks to the door and opens it. "Where exactly?" Her voice carries in the hall, maybe right to Mrs. Boika's apartment. "Where did you fall down the stairs?"

"I hit my face somewhere at the end there. It's not like I can make a map, Ma. It was so fast." I take a deep swig of tea, hoping to end the interrogation. I try not to let her see me trembling.

Ma closes the door and comes back to the kitchen. My lie is just out of reach, but she's too cautious to edge out on this thin branch. She wants me to confess instead, tell her what really happened. But I stay quiet. She takes off her coat slowly, turns to Lila, and crosses her arms.

"*Imagínate.* All those years we spent crawling up and

down crumbling steps in the old place, and look where my daughter falls. That's pretty strange, right, Lila?"

My heart squeezes in the long quiet that follows; I can't breathe. Smoke has snaked over all our heads as Ma waits for her best friend to answer.

Lila stubs out her cigarette and gets up to warm the food.

"It's a strange world, Clara. You know that. "

CHAPTER 23

I stay in my room all weekend, studying myself in the mirror every chance I get. The girl looking back at me is someone new. Mitzi texts me twice to try to make up, but I don't answer. If she saw this girl now, what would she say? My eyebrows are thin, crooked, and mean as a murder. My left eyelid is swollen into a slit, and the whites are demon red. The scrape on my chin makes my face look lopsided. All over, the bruises have settled in, deep and black, even in places no one can see.

"Piddy!" Ma calls.

Piddy's dead, Ma, I want to explain. *Gone. Adiós.* I picture myself like one of those Day of the Dead skeletons wearing a grin.

But maybe Ma already knows, because when I come to the kitchen to see what she wants, she looks at me for a long time in an unnatural quiet, like someone at a funeral. The worry in her eyes is lye on my skin.

"You need some aspirin?" she asks.

"No."

"Don't be stubborn." She points at the knot on my forehead. "That *chichón* has to be giving you a headache, *niña*. At least put some Iodex on it. Or let me press it down with a cold quarter."

I turn around to leave.

"Piedad Sanchez," she snaps.

"*What?*" My voice is loud in the kitchen, suddenly sharper and bolder than hers.

Ma considers the peppers she's chopping and stops, confused by this new girl. Finally, she sighs and points to the trash bag with her blade.

"Take that outside. The truck comes tomorrow. And use the handrail!"

It's quiet on the street as I hesitate at the outside door. Fear is my new best friend. It stands at my elbow in chilly silence. The trash cans are around the back of the house, and the thought of getting there makes my heart race. Anyone could be hiding in the nearby bushes. Yaqui, Vanesa, anyone at all. Even when I close my eyes to steady myself, I can still see Yaqui and her friends. I can practically smell her breath on my neck. This is what it's like to be haunted by spirits — I'm sure of it.

Just as I'm working up my nerve, something rustles in the front yard and makes me jump. It's only Mrs.

Boika, leaning over the stupid rosesbushes, wrapping the branches in burlap for the winter. A plant, she can protect. A neighbor who is being beaten like a dog? Forget it. She straightens up and stares at me through the thorny branches. I refuse to look away or smile. Instead, I let her get a good look at what she let happen. *I hate you, Mrs. Boika,* I tell her with my devil eyes. *Get back to your thorns.*

I finally force myself to get moving and start for the back of the house. I walk faster the farther away I get from the door. In a panic, I toss the bags toward the closed trash cans. An animal will probably make a mess of it, and Ma will pitch a fit. But I don't care; it's the best I can do. I hurry back to the front door, desperate to get inside. Sweat has beaded along my lip. Suddenly I notice something on the sidewalk.

It's pale green and tiny — my jade elephant, or at least what's left of it. The chain is gone, and the trunk is broken off. One whole side is scraped white from being crushed under Yaqui's heel. The sight of my ruined charm makes me angry all over again. I wish I could have crushed Yaqui flat beneath an elephant's foot, abandoned her on the street with no shirt. My eyes well up as I reach for my charm.

"Piddy?"

The voice makes me flinch. I look up to find Darlene. She's probably here to cash in again on my debt for

Yaqui's schedule. I ignored her calls all morning. I haven't been answering my phone. Not for Darlene. Not for Lila. I deleted every message as soon as it came in. But apparently Darlene can't take a hint. She plucks out her headphones and stares in shock. I try to look away and hide my face, but it's no use.

"Holy crap," she whispers.

I snatch my elephant off the ground and straighten up, trying to look natural as she takes inventory of the damage in detail. My bruises feel even deeper with her gawking at them.

"I can't help you with homework today," I say. "I'm busy."

Darlene shakes her head. "That's not why I'm here. I didn't believe it, but I saw . . ."

"Go home, Darlene." I turn for the door, then pause. "What did you see?" Instead of answering, she fishes in her purse for her phone. When she finds it, she scrolls quickly and holds the screen in my face. A spider of dread creeps up my spine.

A grainy phone video starts playing from the web. A crowd of girls is hooting around another girl. It's me, of course, or at least the old me. My stomach plunges as I watch the fight happen all over again. The camera catches one hard slap after another, the tear of my blouse, my hands grabbing to cover myself.

Darlene stops the video just as the me on the screen is pounding on this door, naked from the waist up.

I close my eyes and rest my head against the side of the house. I'm ruined.

"Seven hundred and four hits so far," she says. "I mean views. Sorry, Piddy."

CHAPTER 24

Monday.

I watch the sun come up between the buildings and sidewalk trees, thinking about school. There's no way to hide what's happened, not enough makeup in the world that can cover up what people at school already know.

Yaqui Delgado kicked my ass.

How many people have seen the video by now, I wonder. When I checked last night, there were already comments posted, mostly about my "fine rack." One kid called me a slut. I squeeze my eyes shut to keep from crying again. I imagine walking into DJ. Everyone will whisper, make fun of me, or else feel bad. Maybe even hit me, too, since I'm clearly an easy target.

Ma starts shuffling around the apartment. The shower water rushes through the pipes, and soon after, she snaps on the hall light and opens my door. Her hair is still wet; she smells sickeningly of almond lotion. I lie still as a corpse and squeeze the elephant charm in my palm until it hurts. Finally, she shakes my leg to wake me.

"Time for school," she whispers.

Squinting into the light, I sit up slowly. Everything hurts. The scab on my elbow cracks open.

"You were so restless last night," she says. "You were talking in your sleep."

"Just dreams," I say. One thing is for sure, though.

I'm *not* going back to DJ. Not ever.

"Can you help me or not?"

I'm at Joey's bedroom window. It's an old trick we used when we were little. I was too afraid of his pink-faced father coming to the door. And Joey's mother, so sad and quiet, reminded me of a ghost. Throwing pebbles on the glass was our signal that I was outside and ready to play.

I know it's crazy to be here where Lila might spot me, but I'm counting on the fact that Salón Corazón opens at noon on Mondays, and she's never up before nine if she can help it.

Besides, Joey's my only hope. He's an expert at cutting school for days at a time without too much hassle — which is exactly what I plan to do. Nobody even bothers to report his absences anymore. "They're pretty glad when I don't show up" is how he once bragged about it. Maybe he'll keep me company.

Barely awake, he rakes his fingers through his blond head stubble. I can see he's got circles under his eyes almost as bad as mine. It's probably been another night of fireworks between his parents.

Joey gets a good look at my face and cocks his head.

"Who messed you up?" he asks.

I look away, thinking back to all the times I've seen Joey scabbed over, never once asking about it. How many times his mom waited on the hall steps, red-eyed and shivering. I said hi and stepped past, minding my own business each time.

"Forget it," I say.

"Wait."

A few minutes later, he joins me at the back of the building. He pulls a can of cat food from his pocket, pops it open, and runs downstairs to the basement. He's back in a flash, tosses away the can, and cracks his knuckles.

"You like the city?" he asks.

The subway smells of dust and pee. Joey doesn't seem to mind — not the stink or the cold. The air is chilly enough to make my nose run, and my swollen cheeks feel stiff. A couple of little kids stare at my mashed face from behind their nanny's legs, which Joey finds hilarious.

"I always knew you were a freak, Toad," he says as he ushers me to the end of the platform. Mice dart along the

175

tracks. Six hundred volts are beneath their grimy paws, and still they look carefree.

"Maybe we'll see one fry," Joey says hopefully. "We could bring home barbecue for the kittens."

"Don't be gross." I watch for a minute, remembering something our science teacher told us in eighth grade. "Besides, it won't happen. Their bodies are too small to touch the rail and the ground at the same time. You need a complete circuit."

"Thanks, professor," he says.

The platform is getting crowded, and soon we're squeezed close. He smells faintly of soap, and I'm so tired that I close my eyes and rest my head on his chest. He doesn't shrug me off. Instead, he keeps me warm. If nothing else, being with him helps me avoid weird men with staring problems. You've got to watch your ass in the subway — literally — even one that's been kicked in like mine. I've heard plenty of stories from Lila.

The trains are slow this morning, and people are getting nastier about it by the second. Sighs and pacing, a few people shaking their heads. It's crowded even here at the end, so naturally it doesn't take long before somebody gets rude.

"Get your greasy backpack off me, man!"

A tall guy at the very edge of the platform gives a nasty look to somebody behind him. The tips of his shoes are hanging over the yellow line. I hold my breath, wondering what's next. The two guys he's insulted don't look like the types to back down. One wrong shove and somebody's through. Joey could get more of a show than he bargained for.

Luckily, the platform begins to rumble, and the headlights of the Express draw everyone's attention. As the train pulls into the station, the crowd starts pushing for the doors, not even waiting for the riders to get off. I'm about to join the crowd, when Joey slips his arm around my waist and holds me back. His touch hurts a tender spot near my ribs. It takes my breath away.

"Wait for the next train," he says in my ear, and I shiver. His fingers make a strangely pleasant ache against my bruises as I wait.

The Local arrives a few minutes later — much emptier, and we snag the end seats, where it's just the two of us, our legs touching.

Neither one of us says much as we squeak and sway our way out of Queens. My face is so ugly right now, I don't want him to look at me, but I can feel him staring just the same. I keep my eyes on his boots one stop after the next.

The train starts to go underground to get us across the East River. Everything gets darker and darker as we go. Joey suddenly stands up.

"Where are you going?" I ask.

He opens the back door of our train car — exactly the

way the sign says not to. Before I can say anything else, he steps out, putting one foot on the metal platform of each moving car, straddling the open space beneath. He holds out his hand from the darkness. One of his tattoos is a little swollen, infected.

"Let's ride out here," he says.

I know it's stupid, but at this point, what's *not* stupid? I step out carefully and position myself opposite him. With a sudden lurch of the train, the door slams shut like a guillotine, and we're outside in the darkness. The train gathers speed, and soon we're hurtling through the dark, sparks flying from the wheels as we go. I grip the handles as tight as I can and let my hips go loose enough to sway with the movement of the car, its own cha-cha-cha.

It's just the two of us out here in the dark, and the sound is deafening. Dust and grime fill my nose and mouth as the air rushes past, and every few seconds a tunnel light illuminates us as though we're under strobes. Even in the dark, I can see that Joey doesn't hold on. He just lets out a laugh, taking in my fear as he pretends to lose his footing.

"Let go!" he shouts as we head around a curve.

My hands are sweaty, but I can't let him have the satisfaction of scaring me, even as the train leans and screeches into the turn. Kids do this every day, I tell myself. I've heard of some who even ride the roof like Spider-Man, invincible. I let my fingers go slack and do my best not to get pitched onto the tracks.

It feels like forever, but we finally pull into the station. My hair is windblown and my heart is racing, but as we stop, Joey leans toward me. He rubs one of his fingers along my swollen lip. Eyes open and fixed on mine, he gives me a kiss.

Even when the train climbs back out to the daylight, I'm still breathless with fright and something like love.

CHAPTER 25

Where did the day go? It's all a jumble. People were scrambling to work in every direction, and we had to move fast, even though we had nowhere to be. It's like we were homeless, with a million places to go and not one place we belonged. My head still rings with the sounds of cabs and bikes, the blinking billboards. The dark window at the entrance to Madame Tussauds, where neither one of us had the thirty-six dollars to get in. A smoky pretzel on the library steps, just like with Mitzi. Every preschooler in Manhattan at Toys"R"Us as we roamed the aisles.

"You're dead," Joey said, pretending to shoot me with the green-and-yellow gun he'd made at the LEGO table. I don't mind. Over the years, he's murdered me with all kinds of things: branches, fingers, empty toilet-paper rolls. It gets old.

It's two thirty by the time we get back, hungry and cold. Ma will be calling soon to see how my day was. *Fine,* I'll say. *No problems. Yes, I feel much better.*

I fumble for the keys as Joey waits, chewing his nails. For once, Mrs. Boika is nowhere to be found. I open the door and turn around to say thanks and bye, but he steps inside. If Ma could see this, she'd die — or I would.

"You can't stay," I tell him.

"Why not?"

"My mother would kill me."

"She won't know."

I hesitate just long enough for him to spot the stairs. His eyes look gray in this light, his cheeks flushed. He is, I realize, as beautiful right now as I am ugly.

"It's too early to go home, Toad," he points out. Then he smiles one of his crazy grins and heads upstairs without another word.

Joey never set foot in my old apartment — and I was forbidden to go inside his. Ma declared his place off-limits the first time we heard Mr. Halper smack his wife around. No words, just the rumble of his voice, with her yelps: *Stop it, Frank!*

"No man puts his hands on you ever, you understand?" Ma whispered to me every time they started up.

In the end, she said Joey and I had to be "on-the-block" friends, period, and even then Ma didn't like it. "Like father, like son," she'd say.

I wonder what kind of friends Joey and I are now. I feel like one of those commuters from this morning

181

staring into the black tunnel, unsure of what's coming or when.

I can't say I really mind having him here, even though he looks strange among our things, like something foreign and wrong for the room. He pokes around cautiously, the way a rescued dog might sniff around his new home, wondering whether to trust it.

Then he spots the piano.

"You play?" He throws open the keys and starts his rendition of "Chopsticks."

"No," I say. "Shhh! The lady downstairs will hear."

He makes a rumble on the lowest keys in protest before I close the piano on his tattooed fingers.

I go to the kitchen and put the water on for tea. When I come back, I find him on the couch, toying with my cell phone.

"You got a message, Toad." He props his feet up on one of the boxes we're using as a coffee table. That's when I realize he's not talking about my cell phone but the house phone. It's blinking, and the caller ID reads: DANIEL JONES HIGH SCHOOL. A weariness takes hold of me. The lies I'll have to tell. The plan that doesn't exist for what happens tomorrow or the day after.

Joey follows my gaze to the machine. For a second, neither one of us moves.

"Observe," he says.

I take a deep breath as he presses DELETE to make the words disappear.

Then he stands up and takes my hand.

"Where's your room?" he asks.

I haven't made the bed. The sheets have spots of blood and still stink from ointment. My floor is littered with dirty jeans, sweaty bras. Joey sits down on the edge of my bed and smiles.

I close my eyes as he pulls me close. Or maybe it's not me, but this new girl with the pummeled face and the mouth full of lies. Inside my head, I can hear Ma talking about decency. Lila's words dance there, too. *It's not a game.* But Joey knows what it's like to have to coarsen your hide against someone's punches. Who else can keep me from Yaqui, if only for this day?

He slides me back onto the bed and climbs on top of me. I tell myself that I'm ready for anything, that this lump in my throat is nothing at all. I picture myself in my tight hair and skinny brows.

He takes my face in his hands and kisses each eyelid and my scabbed mouth. He closes his eyes and runs his fingers under my shirt. His touch makes the skin on my arms go to gooseflesh. I don't stop him from working the buttons of my blouse or the hook on my bra. In a moment, my bruised shoulders are bare. I keep my hands at my sides, too frightened and tired to even move as his lips brush my skin at the top of my breasts. His hand moves across my ribs, and before I can stop myself, I wince in pain.

Joey opens his eyes.

"What?" he asks.

His face goes dark as my shirt falls away and he sees all that has happened to my body. I'm mottled in purples and greens, tattooed in crusty scabs. I have bumps and swells where they don't belong.

The corner of his eye twitches, and his mouth turns down as he studies me. After a long minute, he circles the bite marks on my shoulders and chest with his finger, tracing them as though he's following a road map to a place he doesn't want to find. He looks pale, and for a second, I swear he's going to be sick.

I am ashamed under his gaze. There are tears in my eyes, so I squeeze them shut, wanting him to get on top of me again and press me close, wondering what this will be, what it will feel like to have Joey inside me. There will be no way back, but would I want one? I'm nearly a woman, right? Maybe I'll laugh about it lightly the way the ladies at Salón Corazón do. I will make it No Big Deal. *Tears are stupid, a thing of little girls,* I tell myself.

But Joey sits up and moves to the edge of the bed instead. He clasps his hands and stares at a spot on the floor, thinking.

"Don't stop," I tell him, desperate for him to help me feel better. "Please."

But Joey stands up slowly and covers me with my sheet. I start to cry hard, humiliated.

"I'm sorry," I blurt out.

My words are like a hard slap that makes his face contort. I've repulsed him completely.

"Don't say that," he says, eyes blazing. "Not ever."

He hands me my shirt and leaves.

CHAPTER 26

I call Darlene and beg her to mark me excused.

"I can't go in looking like this. Have a heart," I tell her. "Please."

"It'll cost you some physics homework," she says. "A lot of it."

I agree; cheating doesn't seem like such a big deal now, though I've been absent and haven't even glanced at what we're doing in class.

Later, after Ma's gone, I get on the bus and go all the way out to Mitzi's new school to see if I can catch her at lunch. I keep my hood up and try to ignore people's stares. I need so much to see Mitzi and to try to tell her what's happened, even if I'm not sure she's speaking to me. A long time ago, Mitzi and I made a promise about the first time we were with a boy. We'd told each other first about our periods. About the boys we liked. We'd definitely tell each other about our first time. What I never imagined is that it would be like this. Me so torn up and ugly that not even the worst boy she knows would have me.

What will she think about me and Joey? She used to be the one who got stuck walking him to the principal's office every day. She complained that he smelled of onions.

I wait near the bushes when I get there. It's nearly lunchtime, and some of the girls huddle around outside picnic tables, even though it's cold. They wear long-sleeved navy sweatshirts over their plaid skirts. There's a sweet sound to the girls chattering and laughing that I've never noticed before. It's like wind chimes. Mitzi is sitting with Sophia — plain, combed, smiling Sophia — surrounded by their other friends. Of course, Mitzi would like Sophia. She is sunshine itself. I can feel her warmth from here. I watch for a long time, trying to figure out how I'd fit in. In the end, I see that I don't. Mitzi's here now, far away from where I once knew her. She can't imagine a Yaqui or a place like DJ. For her, the worst part of her day is taking a hard quiz.

Eventually the bell rings and they all head inside. I think about Mitzi and Sophia as I head for home, their brightness burning a hole inside me.

Wednesday, I have a close call. I get dressed and head to the Glen Ora to give Darlene my homework before school. I'm waiting by the intercoms when someone opens the door and calls my name.

"Piddy? What a surprise!"

It's one of Lila's customers, Maria Estela. I bagged up her Avon order myself but never realized she lived out this way. Great, the vast network of Avon strikes against me.

"You remember me from the party? I'm Lila's friend."

I swallow hard. "Yes. Hi."

"What brings you to my building?" she asks. I can see her studying what's left of my shiner.

I swallow hard as I spot Darlene coming down the hall toward us.

"My friend lives here. I was picking her up so we can walk to school."

Darlene throws open the door just as Maria Estela fastens her scarf.

"Ah. Well, it was nice to see you. Have a nice day at school." She turns before stepping outside. "Oh, and tell Lila I'm loving the skin-firming mask."

I promise her I'll do just that.

"You have them?" Darlene asks when Maria Estela is out of earshot.

"Here." I shove the answers to the physics homework in her hand and head back home.

When Lila calls me that night to check how school was, I hold my breath, waiting to get busted. The Glen

188

Ora is way past DJ. There's no way I'd ever be there to pick somebody up for school.

"Any more trouble?" she asks.

"No, I'm fine. They've left me alone." There's a long pause.

"I found out something today."

Oh, no. Here it comes. I'm queasy, the way I get on elevators.

"The Halpers might get evicted," she says.

"What?"

"It's all over the building. They're six months late on their rent, according to the widow in 2C. The super put a note on their door."

"But where would they go?" I ask, my stomach plunging again.

"What do I know?" Lila says. "But at this point, I'd be glad to lose that trash. There's too much bad drama in that house! I have nightmares of that woman screaming. It's as much as I can take."

"Joey's not garbage," I say, and hang up.

Darlene stops by after school. She looks worried, and her hands are shaking. "I almost got busted today, thanks to you," she says. "Mrs. Gregory in guidance almost nabbed me pretending to talk to your mother when she accidentally clicked into the line." She tosses her head and throws back her shoulders. "I'm done helping you. I'm not risking anything for you anymore. Besides, your work is getting shoddy. You had two wrong on the stuff you gave me this morning. You have to come in tomorrow with a doctor's note or *something*."

"Can't you say there's been a death in the family?" I ask. It feels sort of true, except for being a flat-out lie.

"Really," she says, bored. "Who's dead?"

"That's private," I say.

"Uh-huh." She looks around at our apartment, taking in every mismatched and scuffed piece of furniture — probably so she can report on it to anybody who cares. "Listen, I've been saying I've spoken to an adult, but you've been out for, like, *days*. It's not like I can keep covering for you. Do you know the trouble I can get in? Jeez. And I don't even think you can even move up to eleventh grade with this many absences. There are *policies*, you know."

"It's not like I'm out committing crimes, Darlene." I motion with my arms. "Does this look like a drug den to you?"

"I wouldn't know," she sniffs. "It could be. But think about this: You're going to get put in moron classes if you don't shape up. At the very least, you won't even be considered for McCleary. You need recommendations for that place, you know."

I set my jaw and lie. "I couldn't care less."

"Suit yourself, then," she says. "Become a loser. But don't say I didn't warn you. If you don't show up tomorrow with a note, you're on your own."

"*Fine*. I'll be there tomorrow."

There's a long pause before she answers.

"Look, I feel bad for you, Piddy, I really do. Who would want to come to school looking like you do and all? But after today, *that's it*." She's out the door before I can even say good-bye.

I've never been lucky, although I've tried, believe me. I don't step on sidewalk cracks, and I haven't owned a black cat, although that's mostly because Ma says we can't afford a pet. Every summer Mitzi and I look for four-leaf clovers in Kissena Park, but I've always come up empty-handed. Once I even begged Ma to buy me a rabbit's foot.

"A dried-up piece of rabbit? *Niña*, don't be silly." She bought me an *ojo de Santa Lucia* at a store in Elmhurst and pinned that little black eye to my shirt instead. "Everyone knows *this* is what really works."

But in the end, not even Ma's remedy helps. As if I haven't been unlucky enough lately, not only is Darlene out sick on Friday, but when my fifth absence comes rolling along the desk, Mrs. Gregory calls Ma at Attronica. Worse, she speaks *español* perfectly.

It's ten thirty in the morning, and I'm watching a

morning show about husbands who cheat on their wives with their best friends. I'm on the couch, wrapped in a blanket, when Ma's key clicks in the lock. She storms in and throws up her hands in disgust.

"You better have a good explanation!"

Thanksgiving is only a week away, the start of the season of frenzy. Ma is still in the Attronica-issued rain poncho she wears on the loading dock, where the stock team passes boxes back like old-time firefighters putting out a blaze. I can see through the plastic poncho that she's wearing her lumbar belt, her only defense against the bad back that she complains about at night. Her hair is damp and frizzy. It's stockroom-meets-madwoman.

"Your school called, Piedad!" she shouts when I don't answer. "You haven't been at school. Why not?"

I can't think of how to answer her, the list is so long.

"I'm sick," I finally say.

Ma yanks off my blanket.

"It's busy at work, Piddy. I had to punch out to come here, and there's no one to cover for me. I have no time for games. Why aren't you at school?"

I cut my eyes at her. "I'm not playing games."

Ma catches my arm as I start to storm off to my room.

"They say you've been gone all week. What have you been doing, eh?" She stares at my faded hickey, and her voice becomes a growl. "Is it this boy again? Who is he?

Have you been bringing him to this apartment?" Ma asks. "Is that what you're doing instead of going to school?"

"No!"

"These new clothes," she continues. "This new attitude. You're acting like a —"

My anger boils over.

"Like what? A tramp? God forbid! That's the most important thing to you. The only trouble is that you're full of shit."

Ma blinks in shock. I've never cursed at her.

"Don't you talk to me like that."

"So what if I brought a boy here?" I continue. "You're not exactly one to talk, like you're some kind of nun." My voice is getting shrill as Ma stands there, dumbfounded and helpless against what I know. "That's right! People talk, Ma. I found out about Agustín having a wife. Very nice. Thanks so much for not telling me that you had an affair!"

"Who told you those things?"

"It doesn't matter. They're true, and everybody seems to know but me. Who are you to judge me? The truth is that you're a little *chusma* yourself, Ma."

In all her life, Ma has never slapped me, but her hand comes across my face hard. I'm so enraged that before I can stop myself, I give her a shove back.

"Get off me!" I shout.

Ma's eyes are wild, her face bright red.

"What kind of devil are you becoming?" she demands.

I grab my coat and head out into the downpour.

"Get back here! Where are you going?"

I run down the street blindly, her words chasing me like bad spirits as I go. *Where are you going? Where are you going?* No matter how fast I go, her voice is there in my ears.

CHAPTER 27

The dark of the subway feels good, even though people look away or even step back a few paces when I walk through. What can I look like, all bashed up and wet? They're leaving room, I suppose, between them and me, a potential crazy. Maybe Ma's right, after all. I'm a devil of some kind, one of Ms. Shepherd's monsters, like the Minotaur roaming my labyrinth.

All day long, I get off at stops I've never heard of and switch trains. I travel uptown through the Bronx and then back downtown and over to Brooklyn, staring at my reflection in the windows as we hurtle through tunnels. I glare straight back at the men checking me out, change trains when one with broken teeth starts to touch himself. I get off at Grand Central. Music wafts through the dusty walkways as I wander past the shops all afternoon. A cello. Someone's squeaky trumpet. Paint-bucket drums. Later, after the station fills with the crisscross of home commuters, I ride pressed against strangers and wonder if Joey is cutting school, too, and if he's somewhere in this maze with me, riding by himself to nowhere as the world goes dark. Will he live here like a track rat, I wonder, when there's nowhere else to go?

Ma calls me all day, but I won't listen to a single message. After a while, I just shut my phone off.

When I finally climb out at our station, it's past ten o'clock, later than I've ever been out without telling Ma where I am. *Serves her right*, I tell myself so I don't feel too bad. It's not like she's never kept secrets from me.

The temperature has dipped, and I'm chilled to the marrow, but I start home on foot. I walk straight through puddles, my hands shoved deep in my coat pockets. The side streets are shadowed by long rows of apartment buildings, alleys in between. One or two people walk by, but mostly things are deserted as I get farther from the bus stops and closed shops. It occurs to me that I'm only a few blocks in the other direction from where Yaqui lives. If I wanted to, I could walk to her building right now, hide in the doorway, jump her the way she did me. I'm a crude thing now, a demon, after all.

Men's voices float through the streets from somewhere nearby — laughter, a few curses. But my eyes are straight ahead. The old Piddy might have been afraid, the way Ma taught her. But I don't care now. *Jump me if you want. Disappear me. Make me a milk-carton kid. Who cares?*

196

As I start to cross the street, I spot a cop car on the corner. I don't get far before I hear its door open.

"Hey."

I turn just as a flood of red and blue lights fills the streets. The cherry top is spinning silently like a disco ball.

"Piddy Sanchez?"

The voices on the street go silent as one of the cops approaches me through the glare. It's only when he's right in front of me that I see it's Raúl.

"I thought that was you." He flashes me a friendly smile, but I don't answer. The cold has turned my thoughts into a thick goop. This is his beat, I remember now.

He signals to his partner in the car, then takes a step closer and lowers his voice. "You okay, Piddy?"

I'm light-headed, frozen. My teeth are chattering.

"Fine," I say.

His head bobs as though we're having a pleasant conversation. His partner is waiting in the car, listening to the crackle of their radio; she tells the dispatch their location.

"Thing is," he says, "it's late, and you have a couple people worried about you."

So, Ma has set the hounds on me.

"Nobody has to worry," I say. "See? I'm fine." My lips are quivering, though.

"Hang on." He goes back to the patrol car and pulls a blue blanket from the trunk. He holds it out to me when he gets back.

"It's cold," he says. "And you're far from your place. How about if we give you a ride home?"

I don't take the blanket. Instead, I shake my head and turn to go. "Thanks, but I'm not going home."

His face looks serious as he steps into my path. I'm suddenly aware of his size, his badge, the gun in his holster. I can see his breath in the air between us.

"Your mother and Lila are worried. They've called me twice." He says it just the way I've heard fathers sound on TV. His voice almost breaks my heart. "Now, let's go."

When I get home, I march straight past Ma and Lila without a word and lock my bedroom door. Lila's voice is low. *Gracias, mi vida.* Ma adds her own stupidities. *She was where? She could have frozen. I don't know what's wrong with her. Teenagers, blah-blah.* I don't even care. I strip off my wet clothes and get under the covers, despite my growling stomach and numb, itchy toes. I'll have to wait for Lila to go home and for Ma to start snoring. Then I'll prowl like the beast that I am and find some food.

Ma tries to turn the doorknob.

"Piedad, open the door," she whispers on the other side.

But all I do is roll over, hate her all over again, steel myself to another night of restless dreams. I'll never talk to that hypocrite again.

CHAPTER 28

"Hungry?"

Ma is sitting at the piano in her pajamas, an untouched cup of tea on the lid above her.

I ignore her completely. It's four a.m., and I've crawled out of bed, starving. I only realize she's there when I'm already holding a whole loaf of bread and a jar of peanut butter.

"Sit down, Piedad." She motions to a spot on the bench beside her.

I don't move.

"We're not going to talk about school," she says. "We're going to talk about your father."

My father. She has never used that phrase before.

"I'm pretty sure I know the story now, Ma. No thanks to you."

"You know, it's not so easy to explain things like this to your kid. You don't know that yet. But it's hard to talk about certain kinds of mistakes."

"Why? Because you'd have to turn in your morality-police badge?" I'm pushing it now, but Ma just takes a deep breath.

"You think I would take a woman's husband on purpose? When you think of me, that's the woman you think I am?"

I don't answer. The truth is that Ma has never done a crooked thing in her whole life. She barely drinks. She works all the time. She doesn't date. Her only crime is being a sour nun.

"You going to say anything?" she asks.

"There's no talking to you," I say. "There's only listening."

"Then, listen."

I close my eyes. All I want is food and my bed, but when Ma has you in a net, it's hopeless. I step into the living room and sit down next to her on the bench.

"Don't," I say when she stands up to turn on the light. "It hurts my eyes."

Ma lights a jar candle we keep on the piano instead. It's our Dollar Store *Virgen de la Caridad*.

"You're right that Agustín was married to someone else when I knew him," Ma says. "Her name was Laura."

I watch the light flicker inside the frosted glass. The virgin's arms are spread wide to calm the frightened fishermen beneath her, but her light makes the chipped piano keys glow garishly.

"But what you *don't* know is that your father never told me a word about his wife when we met. He just swept me off my feet with his church music and the way he talked to me about my own playing. That's how I got this piano, in fact. He had a friend who played on Sundays at the bar inside the New York Hilton. Agustín bought it for me when they were getting ready to update the place. I was crazy with joy." She runs her fingers along the keys but doesn't press down.

"You never play anymore," I say.

"No." Ma shrugs. "This old thing blinded me to everything, and I guess I can't forgive myself for being so gullible. I thought I had met someone worthwhile, someone who really wanted to make me happy. But his gift fooled me; he fooled both Laura and me, really."

I stare straight ahead, but from the corner of my eye, I can see Ma's silhouette in the dark as it comes into sharper focus. She's sitting up tall, her hands folded. I've struggled to imagine her having a boyfriend, much less having sex. But now something else occurs to me. Ma was made a fool of. Suddenly that's harder to imagine than anything else.

"So, how did you find out?" I finally ask.

Ma purses her lips and goes quiet for a long time. Finally she takes a deep breath.

"We were engaged and living together in our new apartment in Lila's building. Agustín had gone home to visit his mother — or so he said. Looking back, I should have known it was a lie. No grown man is so attached to his *mami* — not even a Latin mama's boy. Gifts and money and —" She shakes her head. "Anyway, I was working part-time at Salón Corazón and getting things ready for you. I had your crib and everything.

"But one afternoon, while I was at the shop, a tall *mulata* came in. She said, 'I am looking for Agustín Sanchez's whore.' Imagine it! She was one of Laura's cousins, who lived in Elmhurst. There were rumors, and a few nosy bodies in the neighborhood told her that Agustín was making a fool of her *primita* with another woman. Naturally, she'd asked questions, and soon enough she found out my name and where I worked."

The whole tableau floats before my eyes. Ma, fat-bellied, with her broom, the sting of people's stares on her back. A young Gloria fighting to keep her smile. *This is a decent shop, señora,* she might have said. *We're all good women here. You've made a mistake. Come. Come have a cookie.*

"Then what happened?" I ask.

"I said, 'I'm carrying Agustín Sanchez's child, so careful who you call a whore, *señora*. I'm his fiancée. Now, what business do you have with him?' Then she told me every-thing the way it really was." Ma sighs. "A whole family over there that had nothing to do with me. He never even both-ered to come back to explain. No matter how many letters I wrote to him demanding answers, I think he just believed he could keep two secret families forever. After that, I was furious. I burned every last piece of him I could find." She pauses for a second. "Well, almost."

She stands up and moves the candle and tea to one of the boxes crowding us. Then, from inside the top of the piano, she pulls something out that's been taped inside. I hold it close to the flame when she hands it to me and find a photograph of a handsome guy with slick hair and green eyes like mine.

"You look a lot like him," she says.

It's the only picture I've ever seen of my father, the one thing I've searched for. But now a strange emptiness fills me as I ask Ma the one thing I've always been afraid to know.

"Did he ever really want me, Ma? Does he even know I have his last name?"

When I look at her, I see tears in Ma's eyes, and I can guess the answer. My stomach squeezes into a fist.

Ma leans forward and her voice is a whisper.

"He didn't know what he wanted, Piddy. But *I* wanted you — more than anything. You are the only good thing that man ever gave me."

I stare at the picture in my lap and nod stupidly. Ma wanting me should be enough, but somehow it's not.

"A girl deserves a decent man for a father, but that's not what you got, Piedad, and I'm sorry," Ma says. "The important question now is: Who are *you* going to be?"

She gets up and goes to bed, her tea still untouched.

CHAPTER 29

Lila is the one who calls us with the news early Saturday. It's just before nine o'clock, and with only a few hours of sleep, Ma looks pale and dazed as she listens. I know it's bad news before she even tells me.

"That animal," she mutters, crossing herself. "It's his fault. Are the police there now?"

"What's wrong?" I ask from the couch, where I fell asleep with my father's picture. Ma shakes her head and turns her back, but I follow. "What's the matter?" I say louder.

She cups the receiver and shoots me a look. "*Sio, niña.* I can't hear Lila."

But Lila shouldn't even be up right now, definitely not making calls. I stand right next to Ma. "What's wrong with Lila?"

"*Por Dios*, Piddy. She's fine. There's trouble in the building — that's all."

"What trouble?"

She pauses, considering her words.

"What?" I say again.

Ma lets out a long sigh. "It's the Halpers."

"They got evicted?" I ask.

The whole world goes still as I wait for her next words. "She's hurt."

There's no sign of Joey when I get to the building, out of breath and panting, but there's CAUTION tape everywhere and a squad car parked up on the curb. The ambulance has its lights going, but no sound. A few neighbors are hanging out their windows as they chug their morning coffee. Finally I spot Lila at the corner. She's smoking again, and her hair is tucked under a bandana, like when she's sick. She should be at work by now, but she's still in her stretchy pants and sweatshirt from last night. When she sees me, she tosses away her cigarette butt and looks at me carefully. A whole world of questions about last night is in her eyes, but in the end, she just gives me a close hug, letting me breathe in the smell of cigarettes and her perfume.

"What happened to Mrs. Halper?" I ask. The whole way over, I've been thinking of Joey's mom, thin and quiet, her high voice through the pipes. *Stop it, Frank. Please, Frank. I'm sorry.* I'm thinking of the days long ago when she'd sit on the stoop darning Joey's dingy socks, waiting for Mr. Halper to sober up. *Did he kill her?* I want to ask, but I can't get out the words.

The lobby doors open, and everybody gets quiet as the gurney rolls through. Mrs. Halper is cocooned in sheets, like a caterpillar waiting for her wings. Her face is swollen with bruises, but her skin is so pale that she looks blue.

"What else? He got drunk and beat her until she stopped screaming," Lila whispers, shuddering. "The kid found her lying in the kitchen this morning. His old man was passed out cold."

My stomach seizes up at the thought of Joey.

Just then he appears at the lobby door with a cop at his side. I move behind the telephone pole so he can't see me gawking at him the way he'd hate. His eyes are blank, even further away than they were in my room. If he sees any of us on the street, he doesn't let on. He looks right through the neighbors watching his catastrophe and climbs into the back of the ambulance with the gurney. His face is hard, his eyes straight ahead.

Mr. Halper comes out next, looking like crap, as usual, his wrists bound in plastic handcuffs that look like enormous garbage-bag fasteners. He's blinking into the morning light as if he's just waking up, still in his T-shirt and work pants. Another cop is at his side. They pause at the back of the ambulance, but Joey won't look at his father, not even a glance. The cop whispers something to the ambulance crew, then leads Mr. Halper to the squad car instead.

"*Hijo de buena madre,*" Lila mutters.

206

My head is filled with all the times cops have come on account of the Halpers before. *Nothing is happening. I'm sorry for this fuss. He's drunk — that's all.* That's what Mrs. Halper always said. But now I can't help but wonder: Why didn't she just tell the truth? Why was she apologizing?

My stomach is squeezed into a queasy knot, and my mouth fills with saliva as the ambulance pulls away. Lila slips her arm around my shoulder to steady me, but it's too much.

"Piddy?"

I lean over the bushes and throw up.

CHAPTER 30

I didn't go to the shop with Lila afterward, but she didn't argue. Instead, after the cops left and the neighbors finished their gossip, she tucked me into her satin-sheeted bed, called Ma, and got dressed for work. All afternoon, I sat by the window, playing with the empty perfume bottles and waiting for any sign of Joey. But even late at night when Raúl finally drove me home, Joey still wasn't back.

The church bells of Saint Michael's are tolling the hour in the distance, and a cold drizzle has left my sweatshirt damp as I walk around to the back of Lila's building. The apartment looks just as dark this morning. I told Ma I was going to pick up the challah rolls she likes from the Russian bakery, but I just had to come back to check on Joey again. I toss a pebble and stare at his dark window and wait. Nothing. What if he's not coming back at all? Where will he go? I bend down to reach for another pebble when I spot a cat food tin on the ground near the garbage can outside. It's empty and crawling with ants.

The kittens.

Even with Lila by my side, a familiar spider of worry climbs my spine as we open the dark cellar. The trash cans are lined up outside for pickup day tomorrow and the whole area stinks of trash. Lila is holding the front of her robe closed as she follows me to the storage area, her hair all points. I leaned on her bell until her groggy voice came through. "I need your basement key," I said. "Right away."

"Are you going to tell me why you've dragged me out of bed?" She's holding her nose and eyeing me carefully as I put my ear to the storage-room door and fumble with her keys. Part of me hopes to find Joey here when I push open the door. Maybe he'll be asleep like a cherub on the pissy mattress. Or maybe he'll call me Toad and tell me his mom is going to be all right after all. What I don't want to find is two dead kittens.

The padlock clicks open, and I push open the door. "Hello?" I call, reaching like a blind girl until I find the light cord.

"Rats!" Lila screeches. Two pairs of eyes glow from the corner.

"Shhh!" I scoop up the kittens fast and show her. They're adorable, of course, with big blue eyes and faint orange fur, but I can see they're listless. They let me scratch their chins, too limp with hunger to swat at me with their claws. Cat turds are everywhere.

"What's this?" she gasps.

"The cat had her kittens, and they've been living down here. But now there's no one to take care of them."

Lila's mouth drops open, and she shakes her head slowly. "No, Piddy. We can't keep these. I'm allergic to cats. We need to put them outside to fend for themselves. Don't look at me like that! It's the best we can do, *chica*."

"I think they're sick," I whisper.

She bites her lip, thinking.

"Please, Lila."

Suddenly the basement door creaks open.

"Who's back there?" It's the super, nosing around as usual.

I yank the cord to turn off the lights.

"It's just me," Lila calls. She slips a kitten inside each of her robe pockets and shoves me out before closing the door behind us. My fingers are shaking as I click the padlock back in place. He's standing at the cellar door, his dirty hair damp from the rain.

"This garbage makes quite a stink," she says coolly as we walk by. We climb the steps without waiting for his reply.

CHAPTER 31

This is stupid. I'm sorry & I miss you. That's the message from Mitzi that flashes on my phone on Thanksgiving morning. Then another:

I made the team. First game next Saturday night. Please come.

I'm numb inside. It's like a message from another planet, I think. From a place where things like basketball games still matter.

Joey Halper's father beat his mother nearly to death, I type. *She's still in the hospital.* Then I backspace over the words and close my phone. People like the Halpers are why the Ortegas moved in the first place.

The smell of turkey fills the apartment, but I don't feel like eating. I try to stay out of the kitchen to avoid conversation with Ma. She's mad, even though it's the holiday and we're supposed to be happy. I know it's my fault. There were only two and a half days of school this week because of Thanksgiving, so I stayed home. Unfortunately the secretary called Ma again. "Your child has to drop out and get a job or she's considered truant, ma'am." She threatened to call the Hotline for Educational Neglect if I don't show up soon.

The Macy's Thanksgiving Day Parade has already started. I used to watch it with Mitzi and Lila every year. It's our favorite, especially the Broadway numbers.

The doorbell rings, and I spot Lila shivering outside and holding a large box. It's only ten a.m., but we're going to eat early today — noon — because of Attronica's Super After-Thanksgiving Madness Sale. Ma will have to go to sleep this afternoon for a few hours because her shift for the big sale starts at one a.m. Only the crazies shop then, Ma says, but everybody is on call, anyway.

When I open the door, I find Lila, red-eyed and sniffling.

"Here," she says, shoving the box into my arms. "Your babies cost me three hundred bucks!"

I flip open the lid and find the two kittens — asleep but alive. The sight of them is like a mirage. I watch the rise and fall of their bellies without touching them, so tiny and helpless.

"That good-for-nothing vet is a thief — you know that?" She sneezes and blows her nose. "He told me they were dehydrated. 'So give them water!' I told him. But *no.*

212

They needed IVs and shots and who knows what else." She shakes her head. "You're lucky they're cute."

"Thanks," I say. "I'll pay you back."

"Pay her back for what?"

Ma is wiping her hands in the kitchen doorway. She looks from Lila to me, and then her eyes land on the box I'm holding. "You bring dessert, Lila?"

Lila blows her nose again and kisses Ma on the cheek. "Anything good on the parade yet?" She hurries off to the living room and leaves me to fend for myself.

Ma's not thrilled with our furry guests, but not even she is heartless enough to kick kittens out on Thanksgiving. All morning, we play with them and watch the parade. I beg nonstop until she caves in and says I can keep one—but only one.

"How am I supposed to choose?" I ask, but Ma goes deaf.

Maybe there's hope, though. When she thinks I'm not looking, Ma cuts them tiny pieces of turkey wing and drops it in their box. Even Lila, whose eyes are red and itchy, can't seem to resist them.

"These two fur balls definitely have something to be thankful for," she mutters as I let them walk across the piano keys, too light to even make noise.

When the three of us hold hands before dinner, I bend

my head in prayer. I don't know what Ma and Lila are asking for, but I have my list ready:

"Thank you, God, for keeping these kittens alive," I say. "And thank you for letting me keep them."

"Only one," Ma warns. "*Uno.*"

Then I go to my private list.

Please, God, let DJ burn to the ground before I have to go back on Monday. If that's too much trouble, at least make Yaqui move.

Please, God, keep Joey and Mrs. Halper safe.

Please, God, help me deal with this mess.

CHAPTER 32

Bright and early Saturday morning, Lila lets herself into our apartment. The sound of the door swinging open scares me when I hear it. Ma is working, of course, but she forgot to tell me she finally got around to making Lila her own key. I rush out to the front door in my T-shirt and underwear, expecting the worst.

"You're not ready for work yet?" she says. She's dressed in black pants and heels, her coat flapping open. "Hurry up! Gloria's shorthanded, and it's the Saturday after Thanksgiving. It's going to be Grand Central Station in there!"

Lila heads into the kitchen before I can answer. The kittens are padding around, stalking the cords dangling from the window blinds. They've already gotten stronger in just two days.

"Shoo — you'll have my mascara running in no time," she tells them when they spot her. She pulls a carton of milk from the refrigerator, sniffs it, and pours herself a glass. Then she looks at me.

I stand there stupidly. The truth is, I don't have the energy to be a happy and soothing Alka-Seltzer for Gloria's customers today. Besides, what if Yaqui shows up at the shop?

"I don't feel well," I mumble.

"Maybe you're hungry. You eat yet?" she asks.

"No."

"We'll stop at the deli, then." She glances at her watch. "Shake a leg!"

"I'm not going in today," I say. "I'm busy."

"Busy?"

"I have to find a home for one of the kittens, remember?"

Lila crosses her arms.

"Piddy, I love you more than if you were my own kid, but you're starting to piss me off."

"No, really. I feel . . . sick."

"Mmm . . ." She taps her red nails on the rim of her glass, thinking. "I know what you need: a pick-me-up. Wait here."

She comes back a few minutes later with Ma's makeup case, the one with eye shadows from before I was born.

"Pitiful," she mutters, surveying the contents. "*Da vergüenza*. You'd think I would have rubbed off on her at least a little by now."

"I don't need makeup," I tell her.

But she guides me to a chair anyway and sits close.

"Be serious. Everyone needs makeup." She squeezes the last dollop of concealer against the back of her hand. "Look up."

With Lila this close, I can see the lines around her mouth. Her mascara is clumped in spots, but she has pretty specks of green in her eyes. She frowns in concentration and dabs my eyelid with her pinkie, fading the remaining damage as best she can. Then she reaches for an eyebrow pencil. Her breath is milky as a baby's as she sketches back the old me. I'm grateful she doesn't criticize the butcher job I did.

"Piddy, what's going on?"

I shrug. "What do you mean?"

"I mean you're not Piddy these days. You say no one is bothering you at school anymore, but you won't even go. You're fighting with your *mami* all the time, disappearing. You don't want to work." She stops and takes my face in her hands. "*¿Qué te pasa?*"

"I hate it at DJ — that's all. I'm never going back."

Lila throws back her head and laughs. "*¡No me digas!* A dropout in the tenth grade! *Qué lindo.* And what are you going to do for a living?"

"I don't care. I'll learn to do hair or something. It worked out all right for Gloria, didn't it? She's, like, a millionaire."

"Well, that millionaire still works six days a week, *mija*."

I don't crack a smile. Lila leans back and sighs.

"It's that girl at school, right?" she asks. "Yaqui? She still after you?"

I don't answer, which is the same as a yes in Lila's book.

"*Cristo*, why didn't you tell me sooner?" She shakes her head. "I could have broken her legs for you."

When I still don't reply, she leans in. "I promised you I wouldn't tell your mother what happened, and I haven't, but I need to know what's going on — the whole story."

A cold fear wraps around me tight, but I'm so tired of worrying about Yaqui that I finally sigh and give up.

"There's a video," I begin. "Somebody took it the day she jumped me. Now the whole school has seen it. I was half naked by the end." My eyes fill up before I can stop them. Lila grabs a napkin and dabs at the gray mascara streaks that are starting to form.

"A video," she mutters. "In my day, they busted your lip, and that was that." She closes her eyes and takes a deep breath. Being responsible never comes easy to Lila. "Here's the thing. You still have to go back to school on Monday."

It's like ice water on my head. "No."

"Listen to what I'm going to tell you," she says gently. "You can't let Yaqui What's-Her-Face get her way. She'll never leave you alone if you run now."

"Let her have her way?" My face gets hot, and I push back in my chair. "*Let* her? I didn't *let* her do anything! She jumped me for no reason—and I don't even know why she hates me."

"She *doesn't* hate you."

"Yes. She does." It's hard to keep my voice steady. "You want to see the bite marks she left on me again?"

Lila shakes her head. "She doesn't even think you're a person. For that matter, she doesn't think *she's* a person. You're just the next one in her path. It's not personal. That's how it is where she's growing up. Beat or get beaten."

"And how do *you* know everything about Yaqui Delgado?"

Lila looks at me and shakes her head.

"Because there's always a Yaqui in every school, in every place in the world. I met a few *malditas* along the way myself," she says. "You think I could look like this and not have people hate on me?"

She chuckles and pulls out a stick of blush.

"It's different now," I say as she starts rubbing the cream into my cheeks. My mind fills with the video, shot by shot for everyone to see.

"A little. But at least one thing is *exactly* the same," Lila says.

"What?"

"You know where this Yaqui girl is going to be in a few years if she doesn't change? She'll still be there—same as always in her old neighborhood — a nobody with nothing. And guess what? That's her worst fear. And who knows? Maybe that's what she'll deserve for being a punk and making people feel bad just because she could.

"But you? You're different," she continues. "You're going to be better than that, and that's what kills her, Piddy. *That's* what makes her burn with hate. She can already see you're winning. You're going to get an education and use your brain. You're going to be a *bella persona* with a good job and a nice place to live, maybe even nicer than Gloria's or Mitzi's. You'll get somebody good in your life who's not going to fool you with a hidden wife. And you'll make enough money to take care of your mother when she's old. *Ay*, Piddy, one day you'll be so far away from Parsons Boulevard, you'll think you dreamed this hellhole."

I put my head down and sob.

"I'm still scared," I say.

Lila kisses my head and whispers in my ear. "I know. But it's you that has the *real* strength in all this, Piddy. You just don't know it yet."

She packs up Ma's supplies and stands up. The kittens scatter off to the living room.

"Now get dressed, *niña*. Our customers are waiting."

CHAPTER 33

It's a beehive at Salón Corazón, just the way Lila predicted.
The bells on the door keep jangling with one person after
another. The women are comparing holiday sales from one
store to the next, trading coupons and diet secrets, complaining about which family member ruined their meal
this year. I try to tune everyone out, putting my face in the
hot towels from the dryer when the thought of Monday
makes me want to cry all over again.

Around noontime, my phone vibrates. I don't recognize the number, so I ignore it. When it vibrates again a
few minutes later, I open the text. The words jolt me.

Come outside.

Shit.

I peer through the beaded curtain. I can't see anybody
waiting outside the shop through the plate-glass window. That only leaves the back door, which leads to the
alley. There is no way I'm going into an alley with Yaqui.
My hands are shaking as I go to the employee bathroom.

The window is high on the wall, almost near the ceiling, but it's got opaque glass. The only way to look out is to open it — and it's the crank kind. I close the toilet lid and climb up. I turn the handle slowly, trying to open the window so gently that no one will notice the pane moving. When it's open an inch or so, I finally look outside.

Joey is standing there, kicking at little chunks of asphalt with his boots. He looks scraggly, like he hasn't seen a shower in days. He's staring at his phone, clicking away. My phone vibrates again. I grab my jacket from the hook in the supply room and go outside to meet him.

"What are you doing here?" I ask him.

"Standing. What does it look like?" He blows into his hands to keep them warm. His fingernails, I notice, are filthy. His eyes still have grit in the corners.

I want to ask about his mother, find out where he's been, but I know better than to pry. Maybe he's as embarrassed as I am about what happened; I don't know. I'm trying not to think about being naked under his questioning eyes or his mother's pale skin on that gurney. *Please, God, don't let him be thinking about the same things.*

"I'm going to Pennsylvania," he says. "To live."

I don't know what to say. I can't tell him I'm sad, for sure, or that I care at all about what's next for him.

"What's there?" I finally ask, even though I know it's more about what's *not* there.

"Friends." Then he shrugs. "Cows and shit paddies, too, I guess."

"Appealing," I say, and we both smile.

He looks at his shoes. "I'm leaving tonight."

I look at him for a long time, my throat getting that tight feeling again. Who would have guessed I would ever miss Joey Halper? But it's true.

"You going to be okay?" I ask him.

"Better than here." He loosens another chunk of asphalt from a hole with his heel. "She'll go back to my old man. Who needs that?"

There are a million things I want to say to him. That I hope Pennsylvania is where ten-year-old Joey can come back out to play again. That maybe Pennsylvania will let him be somebody new so he can sit at a table on holidays and say, *Thank you, God,* and really mean it.

But before I can say anything at all, he reaches for my face with his dirty fingertips and looks at me dead in the eye.

"Come with me, Toad," he whispers. "Let's get out of here."

The first *novela* I ever saw with Lila was *El Amor Es Destino. Love Is Destiny.* In it, the girl's lover steals her away from her family in the night. Ma hated that *novela.*

"He's kidnapping her," Ma said. "He should be arrested."

"Shhh! She wants to go. It's so romantic," Lila told her.

All night, I'm thinking of that soap opera and watching the clock. The bus leaves at nine p.m. from Port Authority. I'm thinking, too, of what Lila told me.

One day you'll be so far away from Parsons Boulevard, you'll think you dreamed this hellhole. I've never so much as been to Pennsylvania. I can't even imagine a life there — except how nice it would be to start in a place where no one knows me. No expectations. No chocolate-milk fastball. No Yaqui anywhere in sight.

Still.

I check my phone; no one has sent me a message. Not Ma — busy at work. Not Mitzi — maybe she's finally given up on me. Tonight was her first basketball game, and I wasn't there to see it, so I don't know if Sophia ever managed to make Mitzi any good.

I'm sorry, I text her.

I don't have time for much else. I have to meet Joey. I fold the note I wrote for Ma and leave it on the kitchen table, so she won't worry. Then I grab my bag carefully and pull the door shut.

I can see the glow of Joey's cigarette as I reach the corner where he's waiting. He has on his army jacket, and a duffel bag is slung over his shoulder.

He hugs me tight when I reach him, and I swear I pick up a metal scent on him, something like fear. We both know I can't go with him, but that doesn't keep him from trying to change my mind. The whole ride to Port Authority, he holds my hand and tells me about Pennsylvania. I can tell he's nervous. He jiggles his knees and cracks his knuckles until I beg him to stop.

The station is packed with travelers trying to make their way back home. Joey and I look for the monitors and squeeze through the lines that are spilling out into the walkways. At the gate, with all the seats in the waiting area full, we sit on the floor. That's when I show him the kitten I hid in my bag.

"They got sick of living in your crappy building, too," I explain.

After a whole day working on my feet, I'm exhausted. My eyes feel heavy as I rest my head on Joey's shoulder. I remember when we were little and nothing too terrible was happening.

"Remember when Mrs. Feldman used to send you to my classroom?" I ask him dreamily. Joey was always sent out of his classroom because he couldn't stop "behaving like a baby," according to Mrs. Feldman. His desk had to be alone in the back. My teacher referred to it as Siberia.

"She could never take a freakin' joke," he says.

"You glued shut the class set of dictionaries."

We both start to laugh.

At eight forty-five, there's an announcement.

"Gate Seventeen, making stops in Mount Laurel and Camden," crackles through the speakers. The line is already moving forward. I can smell the bus fumes wafting through the open glass doors as we stand up and gather our things.

Through the glass, I watch people hand their tickets to the driver and get their luggage tagged. Joey's grip on his own ticket has left it blurred and wrinkled, I notice.

"You sure you don't want to come?" he asks.

I pull him close and unzip my backpack.

"Here." I scoop up the orange kitten and slip the little fur ball inside his jacket, where it's warm near his skin.

"Tell him to write," I whisper to the kitten, avoiding Joey's gaze. Then to Joey I say, "I've still got his brother." And then I pull out one more thing. It's the envelope I usually keep in my drawer. I press it into Joey's palm.

"What's this?" He opens it and doesn't say a word. Inside is a thick stack of ones and fives — two months' worth of tips from Salón Corazón.

"In case you need it," I tell him. "And don't blow it on tattoo ink, you dope," I say quickly. "I swept up a lot of hair for that."

When he looks at me, I can see that his eyes are fuzzy.

"Last call for boarding!"

My knees feel weak and I suddenly want to follow, but if I go with him, Yaqui will have taken everything from me. Ma and Lila and Mitzi. Even who I want to be.

226

So, I kiss Joey on the cheek and hug him close enough to feel the kitten squirming. I can feel Joey's breath tickle my neck as he whispers.

"Take care of yourself, Toad," he says. "Run if you have to."

Then he climbs up the bus steps and he's gone.

CHAPTER 34

The walk to school is silent that Monday. Lila is with me. "Just in case," she says, but I'm not sure if she means "Just in case Yaqui is around" or "Just in case you don't go."

It's not even December, and the air already smells like cold metal and snow. I wonder if it's like this to walk to your death. You know, like in prison. Empty. Ready for everything to stop with a prick of a needle, a jolt. Like you're walking in a dream. All I've got to make me feel better today is my broken elephant charm in my pocket— and it's not working too well. The closer we get to school, the worse I feel. I know I'm either going to get beaten up by Yaqui again—or I'm going to have to narc like a loser and probably get beaten up even worse when she finds out.

At the attendance office, the secretary glances tiredly before opening the passbook. Then she gives Lila the once-over, her eyes lingering on her zebra-print pumps.

"Sign her in, please."

Lila is studying the posters on the bulletin board. She smiles innocently and peruses the sign-in log like it's one of her glossy catalogs.

"We've both been a little sick, but it's nothing contagious — don't worry." She signs Ma's name with a flourish. "Have a good day, *hija*." She winks at me, but I won't crack a smile.

Instead, I grab the pass from the secretary and slip away as fast as I can. The clicks of Lila's heels fade in the other direction as I go.

"You'll need this to have any hope in U.S. History next year," Mr. Fink says to the class. He pauses from his explanation of nationalism when I come in and drop the pass on his desk. I try to act like no one's staring, but all eyes are on me as I find my seat, especially Darlene's. I can't help but wonder what they're thinking. Are they making fun of me? Are they remembering me naked in that stupid video? Or can they see that I'm something foreign now, different, a curiosity that doesn't belong in this little bubble of smart kids who still care? They've probably seen the video, gawked at me naked, and been grateful it wasn't them. Maybe some of them think I'm something dangerous that has to be amputated for the sake of the whole.

Sally Ngyuen sits up straight and looks ahead when I sit down next to her.

"Discussion questions, page two hundred and two," Mr. Fink tells us. "And I want answers in complete sentences."

Book, notebook, pencil, I think slowly — the motions of a normal day for normal people. The words at the top of the page blur up, though. I read the words again and again, trying to remember anything at all about how the world connects.

"Piddy. *Piddy.*" Darlene's voice is a whisper.

I don't turn her way. When class ends, I dart out before she can reach me and head out to my next class alone.

That afternoon, Ms. Shepherd pretends not to make a big deal about my return, although she stares at me for a beat too long when I come in. Lila's makeup isn't fooling anybody. Add that to my plucked eyebrows and tired face, and I'm probably a dead ringer for someone from what she calls her sixth-period "zoo."

"Okay, everyone," she says, handing out pages of the literary magazine in layouts. "We were finalizing layouts before the break. I hope you remember that our deadline for the magazine is this Friday. You need to work in your groups to make the final edits for your assigned pages." She looks up at me. "Why don't you join Rob's group, Piddy?"

Rob's group consists of Rob.

I take the empty seat beside him as everyone moves their desks into clusters and gets busy.

"I guess it's lonely at the top," I say, trying to break the ice.

"I'm not lonely," he says. The awkward silence that follows makes me feel like an idiot.

"Look, Rob," I finally say. "I'm sorry I yelled at you that day after lunch. I was freaked out the story was up and —"

"You were scared," he says as he unfolds the layout page for the introduction. "Your eyes were doing that weird jumping thing."

The open page catches my attention immediately. A gorgeous sketch takes up most of the page, and beneath it is his name. When I look closely, I see that it has been done in tireless pinpoints — almost as tiny as pixels. When you hold it at arm's length, the image is of three wolf-faced kids writing on a locker. On the back of their jackets, the word LOSER is written in white letters. I think back to the day somebody wrote on his locker. I guess I wasn't fast enough to spare him, after all.

"You're an artist," I say. "I can't draw anything, especially not animals, no matter how hard I try."

"What kind do you try to draw?" he asks.

"Well, elephants." Which is true. They never look realistic; they always look like Babar. Rob is staring at me, so I keep blabbering. "But these wolves are great," I add. I put down the sheet and look at him. So far I've only known him as a brain in every subject. Now I see he's got other talents, too. "Rob, what don't you do well?"

"People," he blurts out.

"Well, yeah, that's true."

He doesn't crack a smile, and another awkward silence wraps around us.

I start to proof his essay for mistakes, but it's hard to worry about commas. Turns out, Rob's bluntness is funny on paper. I'm almost done when he puts his hand over the text.

"Wait — I'm not finished," I say. "It's really good."

"Your stuff would be better than most of what we picked," he says quickly.

This is not a conversation I want to have, much less with people listening in near us.

"We should edit the rest of this stuff," I mumble, reaching for the next page of layout.

"I hate Darlene's sappy poem, for instance," he says a little too loudly. "I put it near the end."

"Did you say my name, Rob?" Darlene gives us a dirty look from across the room.

"She can be such an ass," I say.

"Everyone is sort of an ass now and then," he says, shrugging. "Sometimes even nice people." He blinks. "You're absent a lot. That's ass-ish."

"You're the one who is being pretty ass-ish right now," I point out.

"See? It happens."

That's when there's a knock at the door. A slant of

light comes in through the opening, and Mr. Flatwell steps inside and scans the room. He motions to Ms. Shepherd. I close my eyes and duck down. Maybe I can play dead like a possum near the trash cans. No luck. His rubber-bottomed shoes barely make a sound as he comes near. I feel him standing next to my desk.

"Hello, Mr. Allen," he says to Rob, who goes from red to purple. Then he turns to me. "Miss Sanchez," he whispers. "Please come with me."

A teacher I've never seen before is waiting in his office when we get there. She glances at me from a seat at a student desk he keeps in the corner.

"Thank you for coming, Miss Castenado," Mr. Flatwell tells her. When he shuts the door, I realize she's probably there as a witness. The thought of Mr. Flatwell getting funny with me is gross, but I guess you never know.

He leans back in his chair and takes me in.

"You've been out for several days, Miss Sanchez. I understand your mother wasn't aware you weren't in school."

I shift in my seat. "She knows now," I say. "And here I am."

"It's nice to have you back," he says without a trace of sarcasm. He's quiet for a while. It's like he's waiting for me to say something else.

"Am I here for a reason?" I ask.

The teacher looks over at me and then at Mr. Flatwell. My tone must be a problem again.

"I've received a report," Mr. Flatwell says. "It has to do with you."

"My mother already knows about my absences," I tell him.

Mr. Flatwell leans forward and folds his hands. "Have you heard of SUSO?"

For a second, I'm confused. "What?"

"SUSO. Miss Castenado runs it," he says, pointing at the teacher. "It's a new program this year. It means Stand Up/Speak Out." He hands me a flyer with a bulldog on it. I recognize it from the guidance office. "Bully-Free Zone," it says.

Miss Castenado clears her throat and rolls her chair closer to us.

"It's an anonymous way for people to report bullying," she explains. "Anyone can send us a form, no questions asked."

The room fills with a silence that hurts my ears. Mr. Flatwell picks up a sheet of paper from his desk, but I don't move my eyes from his face.

"I've received a SUSO report that says someone at this school has been bullying you." He looks over his glasses at me. "Is that true?"

"Who filed that report?" I pull my sleeves down over

my wrists nervously. Darlene made it clear she didn't want to get involved. But I can't think of anyone else who would even know there was a no-bullying program in place.

"The report was made anonymously, but it's obviously somebody who's concerned about you."

Someone concerned about me? At DJ? That's a laugh. But as he waits for my answer, I suddenly think of Rob. How he's gotten me out of tough spots before without me even realizing it.

"What you tell us in this room is confidential," Miss Castenado says. "We can help before things get out of hand."

A poster of a kitten hanging from a tree limb is tacked to the wall behind her. HANG IN THERE, it says. My throat tightens into a wad of sadness. Things are already so out of hand, she has no idea. I'm thinking all at once of Joey and Mrs. Halper and all the days we heard her through the pipes. All those times the cops came and left, empty-handed. *It's all right,* she'd say. *Nothing happened.* She didn't accept help, but maybe she was just too afraid to take it.

Miss Castenado goes to the water cooler and fills a cup of water for me. She puts a box of tissues in front of me, too. I don't touch either one.

"Sometimes we can get the people involved talking," she begins, "and we can help them solve their differences."

"No." My voice is sudden, firm.

Mr. Flatwell clears his throat.

"Last year, you were an A student at your old school." He unclips a wallet-size school picture of me from inside a file folder. I recognize the old school portrait. Ma has one floating in her photo box somewhere. It was taken last September at my old school. I must have missed this year's Picture Day when I was playing hooky. He considers the girl carefully. "I've read your records. It says you were in advanced sciences and language arts. Ms. Shepherd agrees that you have talent." He leans forward. "What's happening here, Miss Sanchez? Something isn't right."

Last year? I can barely remember it. That was when I could sleep at night, dreaming of my elephants and the Sahara. I could feel the rhythm of old salsa records in my bones. I could laugh with Mitzi and plan what we would wear. Agustín Sanchez was my mystery father, someone I wanted to know about. Now I can't lift my eyes or walk the way I want. I have no friends. Not even my own father wanted to get to know me. If there is a way to get that smiling girl back, I don't see it.

The room is spinning now. Talking about a secret is like finding a way out of a cave, isn't it? You can't be sure whether you're going deeper in or climbing free. What's the sunlight and what's just a mirage?

I close my eyes to think as hard as I ever have. It's Lila's voice again in my head.

It's you that has the real *strength in all this, Piddy. You just don't know it yet. One day you'll be so far away from Parsons Boulevard, you'll think you dreamed this hellhole.* Her aspirations for me are blinking above like fireflies just out of reach.

"Miss Sanchez? Is someone bullying you?"

I'm thinking, too, of Rob and his wolf picture for all to see, the way he's still standing despite all the abuse that's heaped his way, even from people who should know better. He sucks at people, and yet he's the most humane.

"If you would give us the name . . ."

The question is, What kind of person will you be? I hear Ma in my ear.

Finally, I pull out my elephant charm and put it on Mr. Flatwell's desk. It has no trunk. The sides are chalky and ruined. It's nothing more than a trinket.

"Yes," I say. "Yaqui Delgado."

CHAPTER 35

Miss Castenado keeps me company through the lunch period until Mr. Flatwell returns. I had a choice to leave the room, but what's the difference? Yaqui is going to know I told, either way. At least now, when Mr. Flatwell brings her in, I'll see her face up close — and she'll have to see mine. We can fight even, for once. The crazy thing is that I may never know what we're actually fighting about. Was it because a boy looked at me? My swishy butt? Or maybe because she's worried I'm better than she is? It hardly matters anymore. All this time, I've been afraid of Yaqui Delgado hurting me, and now it's time to confront her — not in a school yard but in a way that I choose. No matter how she fights, I'll make sure I win in the way that matters to me.

It takes a long time for Mr. Flatwell to return. When he comes back, he has the school cop, Officer Roan, along, too. As soon as Yaqui sees me, she shakes her head, as if she's already thinking about everything she's going to do to me. I still can't quite look at Yaqui directly, but I look *by* her—like looking through a windshield instead of focusing on what's stuck on the glass.

Mr. Flatwell sits down and folds his hands.

"Have a seat, Miss Delgado," he begins.

"I don't know her," Yaqui says, still standing. "I don't even know her."

She's right, of course. She doesn't know me at all, but now I stare right at her, even though my hands are shaking. Yaqui's hoop earrings graze her shoulders. She wears gold rings on her index fingers, and there's a tiny white scar that splits her brow. There are two scabs on her elbows, and for a second I wonder proudly if I managed to do her some damage, too.

"You looking at something?" she snaps.

Mr. Flatwell holds up his hand and gives her a warning look before turning back to me.

"Miss Sanchez, can you tell me what's been happening between you and Miss Delgado?"

I don't say anything at first. I can feel Yaqui's rage in the air around me. She'll find me when no one is looking; I know she will. She'll hit me harder, hate me more, even pound her raging story into my flesh until it's a little part of me I can't let go. She's already made scars I'll have when I'm old. I try to keep myself calm, thinking that maybe it's like Ma says, after all: *God put your eyes in front of your head so you can see forward and not look back.*

I try to focus on what's far ahead — after high school, after all of this has faded a bit. There is going to be an after for me, one that's much better than hers.

I start out quietly, my voice flat as I tell Mr. Flatwell about Vanesa coming to me in the school yard. About her visit to the salon. About Yaqui stealing my elephant charm in the hall. Officer Roan is taking notes. Yaqui keeps interrupting, denying all of it.

"She's lying," she says.

"I'm not." And then I reach across Mr. Flatwell's desk and take his pen and notepad. I write the string of humiliating numbers and letters that have been branded into my brain.

"What's this?" Mr. Flatwell asks me, when I hand it to him. "A website?"

My face is burning red.

"Yes," I say. "A movie, actually. Yaqui and I are the stars."

Mr. Flatwell turns to his computer and types in his access code and the YouTube link on his keyboard, and the video begins to load. The screen is reflected in his glasses, frozen on a frame of the fence outside my apartment. Mrs. Boika is in the window, a group of girls standing around with their backs to the camera.

I feel no shame as I watch the video start to play. This time I don't even cry.

CHAPTER 36

"Someone can walk you out if you like," Miss Castenado whispers as she escorts me to the front doors of the school. "But I'm sure Mr. Flatwell will keep Yaqui in his office for a good while. We've alerted the school-yard monitors, too. And don't worry—we're getting the video offline immediately."

I tell her I'm fine, but I realize this is my new life as a narc. I've seen this maneuver on plenty of court shows. The judge gives the witness a head start so the accused can't break his knees in the parking lot. Or, in my case, the school yard.

I'm about to step out when someone walks by us toward the doors.

"Where are you going, sir?" Miss Castenado asks. "There's fifteen minutes left until the bell."

Rob holds up a pass but stares at his shoes.

"I have a pass for early dismissal," he says. "Dermatologist appointment." He steals a glance at me while Miss Castenado checks it out and nods.

He holds the door open, waiting for me to follow, and I do. We walk to the fence without a word, then he turns and hands me something.

"What's this?" I ask. When I open it, I find a one-page application for McCleary, the science magnet school Darlene told me about.

"See the date?" he says. "Due Friday. Hurry."

I stare at the application, my mind moving in a million directions as he walks away. When I look up, he's halfway across the street.

"Hey!" I call, jogging after him.

He turns and waits, the cold air making his nose run a little. When I reach him, I don't know what to say. Then I blurt it out — Rob-style.

"You told Flatwell that Yaqui Delgado was after me?" My voice sounds more accusing than I mean it to be. I take a step closer and whisper, "Somebody filed an anonymous SUSO report, and I think it was you."

He blinks and shifts his feet.

"This is where you answer," I tell him.

"Yes," he finally says. "You fixed my locker?"

Now it's me who's momentarily tongue-tied. I don't know if it's a statement or a question. "Yes."

Rob gives the briefest smile I've ever seen.

"See you tomorrow," he says.

When I get to Mitzi's house after school, no one is there. She's probably at basketball or badminton practice or whatever sport is now in session. I have to sit on the stoop to wait. It's a quiet street, with almost no cars driving by, so I have plenty of time to think. Mr. Flatwell and Officer Roan say I have to tell my mother what's been happening; I have to bring her to school tomorrow. "There are options for how to handle this," Mr. Flatwell said. *Like what?* I wonder. *The Witness Protection Program?*

I pull the application for McCleary from my pack and read all the questions, wondering if I've slipped too far for them to take me now. Sometimes mistakes *can* mess you up forever, just like Mr. Nocera always warns: screw something up in the beginning of a problem, and your whole answer is wrong. *Is there partial credit in the world,* I wonder, *or just in math?*

I don't know how long I sit there, but finally I hear someone coming up the walkway. I stand up and find Mitzi walking toward me. Thankfully, she's by herself.

"Piddy?"

Her bulging backpack is slung over one shoulder. She smiles and suddenly winces. That's when I notice she has a fat lip.

"What happened to you?" I ask.

"I took a ball to the face in the game Saturday night."

"You win at least?"

"No." Then she juts her chin at the last of my greenish bruises. "What's your excuse? You get run over by a truck?"

"More or less."

There's an awkward quiet.

"You get my message?" I ask.

She nods.

"I wanted to come, but I couldn't," I add.

"Why not?"

I shrug. "There's been a lot going on."

For a second, neither one of us says anything. Then Mitzi reaches inside her jacket for the key around her neck and unlocks the door.

"Well, then, you better fill me in."

Just then, my phone vibrates, and I check the message. Relief floods through me.

"What?" Mitzi asks.

I hold up the screen to her. It's a picture of Joey and the kitten in someone's kitchen.

She looks closely, and then her eyes go wide. "No way. Is that who I think it is?"

"Yep. We've got a lot to catch up on," I say as we step inside.

CHAPTER 37

Maybe we only tell our scary secrets when we have no choice. It takes me hours to get the guts to call Ma, but Mitzi is right there beside me when I call Attronica.

"If you don't do it now, you'll lose your nerve."

They page Ma and bring her to the phone.

"Meet us at Corazón at nine tonight," I tell her. Mitzi nods encouragingly. She thought a public meeting place would be smarter. "Tell Lila to wait, too."

"Why would I go there?" She's out of breath. "I'm exhausted, Piddy. I just want to go home."

"Just meet me and Mitzi there after work," I say. "I have to talk to you, Ma. It's important." I hang up before she can argue.

By the time we get to Salón Corazón that night, they're already waiting. Mitzi and I walk up the block and peer inside the shop. It's past closing time, and the door is locked tight, though the grate hasn't been dragged down. Lila and Ma are talking with Gloria like old friends. They're sitting on the chairs with the dryer hoods flipped back, and Lila has kicked off her shoes. Still, I can tell by the way she keeps glancing at her watch that Ma is distracted.

When I knock on the glass, Gloria spots us and hurries over to unlock the bolt.

"There you are. *¡Qué frío!*" she says, shivering as Mitzi and I step inside. "We went from fall to winter like that! Come in, come in! And, oh, my goodness, is that you, Mitzi Ortega?"

There's a flurry of fuss over Mitzi, kisses and hugs. Finally, when things fall quiet again, Fabio starts his normal growling welcome. He's wearing a sheepskin sweater to keep him warm. Gloria scoops him up under her arm and pats my cheek.

"I was just telling your *mami* that I want her in here one Saturday. I'll open up at eight a.m. sharp so she can get to work on time," she tells me. "I'll give her a nice haircut, on the house. Make sure she comes." She smiles sweetly. "But now I'm going to do the receipts, *mijas*. Why don't you come help me, Lila? And Mitzi, come on back. I want to hear how it's going in Long Island. That mother of yours hasn't called or anything! She's forgetting us, eh?" Her voice trails off in happy chatter as they disappear into the back room.

Ma looks around uncomfortably.

"It's weird to see you here," I tell her.

"The place hasn't changed a bit." She's quiet for a few seconds, thinking, I'm sure, of that day when she found out about my father. I can't help thinking of him either, but now it's different. He's not someone I want to miss anymore; he's just someone who didn't want Ma and me in his life, for better or worse.

Ma's voice shakes me from my thoughts.

"I'm not here for a tour, am I? Lila won't tell me anything, so I know it's serious. What is it?"

"It's about me and school," I say.

"Oh, Piddy. What's happening now?" Her face is worn with worry.

I talk slowly, without looking away from her. Ma doesn't interrupt as I tell her why I haven't been going to school. She closes her eyes and listens when I get to the part about Yaqui jumping me. She doesn't even make a peep when I list all the places I went when I skipped. She just presses her lips together and nods. The only thing I leave out is Joey. There's no point in setting a match to the gunpowder — and besides, he's making his own way now.

"Mr. Flatwell wants you to come to school tomorrow, Ma. He said I have options."

"What does that mean?"

I shrug. "I don't really know." Then I feel inside my

pocket and pull out the application for McCleary. "I hope this is one of them, though."

Ma scans what I've written and gives me a questioning look.

"It's a science magnet school I want to apply to, Ma," I explain. "It gives me some college credit, free." I take a deep breath. "Because I'm thinking I want to work with animals, like a field vet. I want to learn about elephants, actually. . . ."

"Elephants," she repeats.

I try to read Ma's expression, but I can't. "Yeah. Maybe." I dig in my pocket for my elephant charm and dangle it between us. "Remember this? Yaqui crushed it."

She looks at the charm and then back at me, mute. When she stands up, instead of telling me my idea is crazy, Ma pulls me to her and hugs me so tight and for so long that I can feel her heart beating in her throat. It's so pure that it takes my breath away. It's as if she's pressing all her strength through my skin and into the marrow of my bones.

"Ma?" My voice is muffled against her neck.

"What?"

"No tirades about *chusmas*, okay?"

She hugs me tighter still.

CHAPTER 38

Overnight, we get the first light snowfall of the season — much earlier than usual. Ma bundles herself up as though we're going on an arctic expedition. She hates the snow and cold, finding absolutely nothing pretty about branches covered in white. On days like this, she usually gives a moody speech about how even when it was winter in Cuba, she still didn't have to wear a coat, let alone boots, a hat, and mittens. But today, as we get ready to see Mr. Flatwell, she doesn't complain. She doesn't even get on Lila's case about her decision to wear new high-heeled boots. The three of us trudge down the block, arm in arm so Lila doesn't slip. The only sound is the crunch of snow beneath us.

When we get to the office, Mr. Flatwell is already waiting for us. The school looks deserted this early. Not even the secretaries are in.

"This way, please," Mr. Flatwell says, leading us through a labyrinth of dark offices until we reach the principal's conference room. He clicks on the light and motions to three seats on one end of the fake-cherry table. "Have a seat."

He takes his spot across from us, lays a file on the table, and folds his hands. Ma doesn't take off her coat.

"Thank you for coming in today," he says. "Miss Sanchez, would you make the introductions?"

I do as he says. Lila squeezes my hand under the table when I introduce her as my aunt. Mr. Flatwell nods politely, and it suddenly occurs to me that he's the first man I've ever met who doesn't smile stupidly at Lila. He clears his throat and gets started, his eyes on Ma.

"I am assuming that your daughter has explained that there have been a few problems at school this year."

"A bully picking on her for no reason," Lila says.

"Yes, and of course she's also been truant."

Ma's eye twitches a little, but she doesn't say anything.

"I had a good reason," I point out.

"You did," he agrees. "But it's still a problem you have to solve. With all these missing days, it will be hard to make up your work."

I give him a sour look, knowing he's right.

"Piddy has never had any problems at school before, right, Clara?" Lila's voice is sharp. "What kind of place is this that lets a bully ruin things for a good kid like her?"

"It's a big school, Mrs. Flores."

"Miss," she corrects. "And so what if it's big?"

"Excuse me. *Miss* Flores." He leans back to explain. "It helps to think of it this way: On any given day, we have about five percent of the student body that makes trouble. That's a small percentage, correct? Unfortunately, it's not a small number of people for the staff to keep track of. In a school of twenty-five hundred students, like ours, about fifty students have parole officers or other problems with the law. Those problems come to school, too. We do the best we can, but sometimes it's not enough."

"When did schools become a place for *criminales?*" Ma asks, slipping into Spanish for a word. "She's here to learn."

Normally I'd be embarrassed by anything Ma had to say, but it's a fair question.

"We have to give every child the benefit of the doubt and offer an education through age sixteen," he says. "Even to the ones who give us trouble."

"Even when they assault others?" Lila says.

He's silent for a moment and then he looks at me. "The good news here is that we also have ninety-five percent of the student body made up of basically decent kids. And one of them was smart enough to report the bullying to us."

"Rob Allen," I say.

He doesn't take the bait.

"I can't confirm or deny the source," he says. "But with a report, we can apply for a suspension. That is, if you confirm it and press charges."

I swallow hard. Yaqui suspended on account of me. I'm dead.

"A report? With the *policía*?" Ma looks scared.

"Yes. A formal charge of assault with the police. We can help arrange that for you."

Ma's face goes another shade whiter.

"How does that help me?" I interrupt.

"It creates a record that can be used in court. Yaqui will have to face the charges, and she may be expelled." He stares at his hands uncomfortably. "The video will help your case tremendously."

My mind is racing over the possibilities. What if she's not expelled? And, as I found out, she can always find me outside of school, which is even worse.

Lila sits up taller and pipes up, as if reading my mind.

"You know that girl will try to jump Piddy again as soon as she can — and I'm not going to let that happen, Mr. Flattop."

"Lila," Ma mutters.

"Flatwell."

"What?" Lila asks.

"My name is Steven Flatwell."

"Mm-hmm," she says, arching her brow.

"I wouldn't advise taking action yourself, Miss Flores.

252

It would be an unnecessary complication." He glances at me. "And maybe not the best example."

"Lila is an excellent *ejemplo* for Piddy," Ma cuts in. She gives Mr. Flatwell a dirty look. "You need to make that bad girl gone for good. Where are her parents?"

He leans back, looking a little tired. "Parents are not an available resource to us in this case," he says carefully. "I wish I could say that we could remove the child forever, but it's not as easy as it sounds. Also, it would be an incomplete solution. To keep Piddy truly safe, we'd have to expel not only Yaqui but her entire social group as well, which is highly unlikely."

As soon as he says it, I know he's right. "You said I had options," I say. "But this sounds like I'm trapped."

"You do have options. There's something called a safety transfer."

"What's that?" Ma asks.

"We remove the victim to a safer school. We would apply to the superintendent for your daughter to return to her old high school, even though she lives out of zone." He opens my chart and looks it over one more time. "The receiving principal would have to agree, but she was a successful student there last year. I don't think there would be a problem in this case. If approved, Miss Castenado in guidance would be in contact with the new guidance counselor to make sure the transition goes smoothly."

"You mean I can leave DJ?" I ask.

253

"You can request to leave DJ. I can't guarantee anything."

Lila frowns. She wants me to stay and fight. It's what she understands — it's how she gets through the world.

"The wrong person is paying the price for this mess," she fumes. "The wrong person is getting kicked out."

"No one is being kicked out," Mr. Flatwell says. "It's not perfect, but it's the best solution I can think of for your niece."

The secretaries have started to arrive, and through the window, I can see kids starting to gather in the school yard. Bile rises in my throat.

Mr. Flatwell glances at his watch and turns to Ma. "I can give you some time to decide what you want to do. You can call me with your decision tomorrow."

I grip the edge of the table. It's not fair that I have to upend my life because Yaqui is bloodthirsty. But so what? Think of how unfairly things turned out for Ma with my father — and how she survived anyway. And how about Joey and his mom? Is it fair to be seventeen and on a bus by yourself to get away from your family? *Run if you have to*, he told me.

"We don't need any more time," I say, glancing at Ma. "I can make this decision for myself. I want a transfer."

CHAPTER 39

I've been thinking lately that growing up is like walking through glass doors that only open one way — you can see where you came from but can't go back. That's how it is for me, anyway.

I haven't seen or heard from Yaqui or her crew since I left DJ last winter. She's probably found someone new to hate, or maybe she's dropped out. And here I am, right back at my old school, where everything is how I left it. The lunchroom, where I used to eat with Mitzi. The teachers who still know and like me. My classmates, who don't know what happened to me with Yaqui or who I became after. I ought to be able to forget DJ and get right back to normal, but somehow I can't. Everything else is the same, but I'm not.

These days, I walk through the halls with my friends, but at lunchtime, I find myself looking over my shoulder. I think twice before I go into a school bathroom alone, even though I know it's safe here. After school, I hang out at Lila's, not just because I want to but also because sometimes I'm still scared that Yaqui will be waiting for me again. Mrs. McIntyre, the guidance counselor, says it will take time. "Trauma takes a while to work through," she told me. "Be patient."

I did send in my application to McCleary, though — right before I left DJ — and I promised Rob that I'd let him know if I got in. McIntyre and Flatwell wrote character reference letters to help, but who knows? Sometimes it's strictly about grades — and mine took a bad hit last semester. For now, I'm catching up on my work — and trying new things when I'm up to it. Just this week, I got a flyer for the school magazine. *Looking for staff,* it said.

Our first meeting is next week.

Ma doesn't tell me she's coming. The door jangles at Salón Corazón on Saturday, and when I look up, there she is. She didn't take Gloria up on the early morning offer, so I figured she wasn't coming at all.

"What are you doing here?" I ask. "Shouldn't you be at work?"

She shrugs and looks around a little awkwardly.

"Oh, I took the day off," she says.

"A day off?" I say, alarmed. Maybe she's dying or

something. Before I can ask about it, Gloria rushes over with arms open wide.

"Clara! You came!"

"I don't have an appointment," Ma says.

Gloria waves her hand in the air as though it's a technicality.

"We can always work in an old friend." She points at one of the hairdressers. "Mirta here has a spot in a little while." Then she winks and calls out to the back of the shop.

"Lila! Hurry up! Your next customer is here."

Lila appears, tying on her apron. She comes to a halt when she spots Ma.

"She says she's taking the day off," I whisper.

"Is the world about to end?" she asks.

Ma gives her a look. "Are you going to wash my hair or not?" She clears her throat. "It's a special day, and I want the works."

Lila arches her brow. "Oh?"

The other customers are looking at us curiously now, and Ma is blushing. She unzips her jacket and reaches inside. Then she hands me a large yellow envelope. "For you."

The return address is the school crest for McCleary. I drop my broom and tear the envelope open. My eyes jump right to the boldface type.

"I'm in for the fall!" I shout. "I'm in!"

"I know. It came yesterday," Ma says.

"You read my mail?"

"Don't give me that look. You slept at Lila's, and I couldn't wait all night to find out. Besides, if they said no, I was going to burn the letter and march down there to change their minds." She gives me a tiny grin. "Luckily, they were sensible."

"I knew you could do it!" Lila cries out. "You've always been a genius! Tonight we celebrate!" Then she looks at Ma. "Uh-oh. Gloria! Where are the Kleenex?"

"I'm fine," Ma insists with a sniffle. "It's all the perfumes in here. . . ."

But Lila just rolls her eyes and pulls her close.

"Crying in my shop?" Gloria says, handing over the box of tissues. "Impossible! It's not allowed. This is a happy day! What we need is some music."

One of the manicurists fishes for the case of CDs under the front desk and pulls out a handful of possibilities. Everyone starts calling out their suggestions.

"Such a racket!" Ma mutters, sitting down in one of the chairs.

"I'll handle this," I say. I flip through quickly and pick out an old one that I pop into the player.

In a few seconds, the music starts. Lila poses like a flamenco dancer and starts to clap out the *clave*.

1-2. 1-2-3.

One by one, everyone joins in, and then the first notes of the piano sound.

"I want to be able to play this, Ma," I say over the beat. "Teach me."

"I haven't played in years," she begins.

"Who cares? I won't know the difference," I tell her.

Ma sighs but smiles. "I guess I can teach you a few things — but you'll learn the classics first, understand?"

Lila grabs a smock and shakes it at Ma like a bull-fighter's cape. Then she does a little spin and grabs Ma up to dance.

"*¡Vamos, Clarita!*"

One by one, the customers climb out of the chairs and join in to dance. "Look at this!" Gloria says, beaming. "We've become a dance hall!"

After a while, I start to dance, too. I shimmy my chest and rock my swishy bottom like no one's business. Even Fabio looks like he's doing a cha-cha as he darts cautiously in between everyone's legs.

1-2. 1-2-3!

"*¡Baila,* Piddy!" Lila shouts as she leads Ma to my arms.

And I do.

Ma's face is shiny with sweat, and her smile spreads ear to ear. We churn that floor, on fire, until we're laughing, and all of our sad days are like faded bruises, almost forgotten. The music is thumping, luring us with its trumpets

259

and sexy trombones. Ma spins me and my arms go wide to the world.

"*No pierdas la clave,*" she whispers to me. Don't miss the beat. She hugs me close when the music ends.

And I know I've found my rhythm at last — strong and simple, constant and mine.

ACKNOWLEDGMENTS

With great appreciation to the following people:

Eric Elfman, Lia Keyes, and Veronica Rossi for their careful reading and thoughtful feedback as I worked on this manuscript

Ada Fernandez McGuire for answering so many questions about school discipline

Jen Rofé, my agent at Andrea Brown Literary Agency, for taking care of business

Kate Fletcher, my wonderful editor, and the whole team at Candlewick Press for the many ways they continue to make me a better writer

And most of all, my family for loving me and for always believing.